MUTUAL ATTRACTION

When Talia followed her young sister Serine to Lanzarote, Dervan Deville told her she was an interfering busybody. Surely Dervan should understand that Serine was too young and immature to live abroad on her own—especially with a wolf like him about! Serine was definitely smitten, but Talia didn't trust Dervan an inch, which was just as well since, when he turned on the charm, he was practically irresistible ...

MUTUAL ATTRACTION

Mutual Attraction

by

Margaret Mayo

Magna Large Print Books
Long Preston, North Yorkshire,
England.

British Library Cataloguing in Publication Data.

Mayo, Margaret
Mutual attraction.

A catalogue record for this book is available from the British Library

ISBN 0-7505-1464-7

First published in Great Britain by Mills & Boon Ltd., 1990

Published in Large Print 1999 by arrangement with Harlequin Books SA

Magna Large Print is an imprint of
Library Magna Books Ltd.
Printed and bound in Great Britain by
T.J. International Ltd., Cornwall, PL28 8RW.

All the characters in this book have no existence outside the imagination of the Author, and have no relation whatsoever to anyone bearing the same name or names. They are not even distantly inspired by any individual known or unknown to the Author, and all the incidents are pure invention.

CHAPTER ONE

'Rosalind, this is Serine's sister. I'm half out of my mind with worry. She's left a note saying she's gone to live with some man or other—I didn't even know she was seeing anyone. Do you know anything about it? You don't ... I see ... Thanks, yes, I will. Goodbye.'

Talia dropped the phone back on to its cradle and slumped into her seat, her grey eyes agitated, her fingers raking absently through her long chestnut hair. Who else was there to ask? She looked again at the note in Serine's round black handwriting.

> Talia, I'm going away with the most fantastic man. He's amazingly rich and he's offered me a job. Don't worry about me, I know exactly what I'm doing.
> Love, Serine.

Don't worry! Talia crumpled the note in her hand and threw it across the room. *Don't worry!* Hell, she'd been worrying about her sister for the last nine years—ever since their parents died.

Serine had been born fairly late in Mr and Mrs Winslow's life, when Talia was already ten, and they had indulged her shamelessly. Coupled with the fact that she had a wilful nature, it meant that Talia had her hands full once they were left on their own. She loved her sister dearly and wished she wouldn't keep causing her these headaches. Late nights and noisy parties were bad enough, but actually running away—and with a stranger! This was the last straw.

She almost felt like letting Serine get on with it. At eighteen she was technically an adult. But she still wasn't really mature enough to cope with something like this. It might seem like an adventure to her at the moment, but if things went wrong, if this man was less than honourable, then who did she have to turn back on?

Talia went upstairs to Serine's room, pulling out drawers and opening cupboards, looking for something that would give her a clue. But nothing. Her diary, handbags, everything, had gone. All her clothes—the lot. It was as though she had never lived here.

The more she thought about it, the more Talia realised what a blind, stupid idiot she was. There had been an air of excitement about Serine over the last few days that should have told her something was happening. How could she have ignored it?

Normally Serine boasted about her boyfriends; Talia tired of hearing it. But this one, this *man*, had not been mentioned. How old was he, for heaven's sake? What sort of a man was he, that he could take off with an eighteen-year-old?

Serine had been going out a lot and often getting in late, but Talia had accepted her explanation that she was at Ros's. Rosalind Russell was Serine's best friend. *But now Ros was saying that she hadn't seen Serine in weeks!*

So who else could she ask? She had phoned all her sister's friends and none of them knew anything about this mysterious man. Talia blamed him as much as Serine. He had no right enticing her away from home. The very least he could have done was come to see her. Though she guessed Serine was behind that. Serine could be very secretive if she chose.

Then suddenly Talia recalled an incident that had happened a few weeks ago and up till now she had forgotten. Serine had been to a Hallowe'en party, returning flushed and excited and talking about 'the Devil'. 'He wore the most fantastic costume you've ever seen, and he had these deep, deep black eyes that looked into your soul!'

Talia had dismissed it as sheer nonsense and the party hadn't been mentioned again, but now she realised that it had been about this time that Serine had begun seeing her friend Ros so often. Except that it had not been Rosalind she was going out with. It had been this man. The Devil!

Another phone call and Talia had his name. Dervan Deville. An eminent architect, single, handsome, rich, and in his late thirties. Talia's heart fell into the soles of her shoes. He was old enough to be Serine's father. And the very type Serine had fantasised about marrying!

More digging turned up the fact that he and a female companion had left London Heathrow for Lanzarote early that morning. It had to be Serine. Talia was dismayed and furious. She had not once envisaged them leaving the country. A job, Serine had said. What sort of a job would she be doing in Lanzarote, for heaven's sake? How could Serine do a thing like this?

She booked a flight for the following day and spent a sleepless night worrying. She had no address on the island, but Dervan

Deville was developing a new holiday complex near Puerto del Carmen, so he would surely not be difficult to find.

The four-hour flight felt like ten. The couple she sat by were on a belated honeymoon and virtually gave her their life story. Talia told them she was visiting her sister, but no more, and wished they would leave her alone.

The green and white airport, running parallel with the beach, was hot and busy, the taxi ride endless, and the task of tracking down Dervan Deville tiring and time-consuming. Talia's temper deepened by the minute. She saw nothing around her, none of the mountainous volcanic beauty of the island. She was in no mood to appreciate scenery.

When she finally found the office from where he operated it was empty except for a woman cleaner, but he apparently had a villa on the island, and the woman gave her the address.

A short taxi ride took her to it. It wasn't

a big place, but it was impressive, set a little way back from the road and away from other houses, with a view of the sea in the distance. As she mounted the steps up to the front door Talia's heart began to pound. What sort of a man would she find? What sort of a man enticed away nubile young girls without even contacting their families?

Her worst fears were realised when Serine herself opened the door, dressed in a slinky strapless green cocktail dress that Talia had never seen before. It emphasised the colour of her eyes and complemented her deep auburn hair. Serine was five feet nine, three inches taller than Talia, and she had never looked so elegant or so beautiful.

Serine's mouth fell open when she saw her sister, and she was instantly on her guard. 'What are you doing here?' she demanded.

Hovering behind her was Dervan Deville —at least Talia assumed it was he. And she could immediately see what had attracted her young sister. He was the sort of man you rarely met. Not strictly handsome, but with that certain something that appealed to women. Nothing you could actually see, but an air about him, a charisma that was like a magnet, and it was this fatal charm that had been Serine's undoing.

Talia drew her eyes away from his black intent gaze and answered her sister. 'I've come to take you home.'

Two deep lines chiselled the man's tanned brow and, stepping forward, he put a hand on Serine's shoulder. A too familiar touch, thought Talia, her blood boiling. 'Exactly who is this?' he asked.

Talia wanted to scream at him to take his hands off Serine, but instead she jutted her chin. 'I'm—'

'This is Talia,' cut in Serine. 'My sister.'

A thick black brow rose. 'And a very bossy sister, by the look of it.'

'She's always trying to make me do things I don't want to do,' said Serine, turning to him with just the right amount of pathos in her voice. 'She won't let me make any decisions for myself.'

Oh, Serine, thought Talia, what are you saying, what are you doing? This man isn't for you. He's far too old and sophisticated.

'And do you want to go back to England?'

'No,' answered Serine at once, using her beautiful green eyes to their best advantage. 'Of course not.'

He looked coldly at Talia. 'Do you hear that? I'm sorry if you've had a wasted journey. Goodbye, Miss Winslow.' And he closed the door.

Talia could not believe he would be so rude, and she stood there for a moment like a mindless idiot. Then she sprang back to life and pounded her fists on the wooden panelling. How dared he dismiss her so arrogantly!

This time Dervan himself opened it, and of Serine there was no sign. 'I'd like to speak to my sister,' Talia said, chin high, grey eyes challenging.

'Your sister does not wish to speak with you,' he replied coolly.

'That's as may be, but you must let me see her.'

'Must? *Must,* Miss Winslow?' His tone suggested she had a nerve, speaking to him like that. 'Serine has told me how you keep interfering in her life, and as far as I'm concerned, unless you have some very good reason for wanting to see her, and I repeat, *very good reason,* then you're wasting your time.'

Dervan Deville was well over six feet, an imposing man, both personality-wise and physically. His hair was thick and black and over-long, brushing the collar of his white shirt. His lips were full and sculptured, looking as though they had been chiselled out of his face, and at this moment they were drawn into a grim line. His nose was straight and there was a decided arrogance about him that stuck in Talia's throat.

'I don't know what your game is, Mr Deville,' she said coldly, 'but you had no right luring Serine away from home. No right at all.'

'Really?' he asked, a faint hint of a mocking smile curving his lips.

Talia could have hit him. Only with difficulty did she keep her hands at her sides. 'Yes, really. Serine said something about you offering her a job, but from what I can see that was purely bait so that you could get your dirty hands on her.'

A glint of anger came into his eyes at her strong words, a muscle tensed in his jaw. 'Miss Winslow, I warn you to be careful what you say.'

Talia eyed him bravely, her chin characteristically high. 'For what other reason would you entice my little sister out here?'

His eyes narrowed warningly. 'Entice her I did not. I offered her a job and she accepted it. It was as simple as that.'

Talia felt for the first time the full impact of his gaze. It was as though someone had run a sliver of ice all the way down her spine.

'What I didn't realise,' he went on, 'was that she had an interfering sister who would chase all the way over here to fetch her back. Hell, surely she's old enough to be allowed a life of her own?'

'I really would prefer to come inside and discuss this, Mr Deville,' she said, still holding his gaze, determined he would not get the best of her.

He looked at her long, hard and cold. 'Very well. Though it won't get you anywhere.'

Talia's heels clattered on the marble-tiled floor as she followed him into his sitting-room. It was simply but expensively furnished, though Talia gave it no more than a cursory glance.

Serine hovered anxiously near the window, and Talia went straight towards her. 'Serine, we must talk,' she said urgently.

But with a defiant glance Serine moved across to Dervan. He put an arm gently about her shoulders. 'It's all right, you don't have to speak to your sister. But I think I ought to have a few words with her myself—alone. Would you mind leaving us for a moment?'

His attitude had changed completely, and it set Talia's teeth on edge. There was a suggestion of intimacy between them that worried her deeply.

'No!' Serine cast Talia a look enough to kill. 'I know what she's going to say. She's going to tell you things about me that aren't true. Why don't you just make her go home?'

'Because she's come a long way, and I think the least I can do is listen to her,' he explained patiently.

Talia could hardly believe he was saying this. If she hadn't insisted he would have sent her away without a moment's hesitation. But she added her pleas to his. 'Please, Serine, just give us a few minutes. I'm here because I care for you, not because I want to spoil things for you.'

'You always spoil things!' said Serine petulantly.

Dervan's arm tightened even more protectively. 'Just a few minutes, hmm? I'm on your side, don't forget.'

Serine smiled and touched her hand to his cheek. 'Very well, but don't let her talk you into sending me home, please, Dervan.'

'I won't,' he said softly.

As Serine walked from the room she glared at Talia, and Talia wanted to go to her and hold her and tell her that she was making a fool of herself, that this man was only out for what he could get, and please, please, would she come home. But she knew these sort of tactics would get her nowhere. When Serine made her mind up about something it took nothing less than an earthquake to change it.

Once the door was closed Dervan Deville turned his attention to Talia. 'Sit if you wish.'

‘No, thanks,’ she said, adopting the same abrupt tone.

‘Then I suggest you tell me exactly why you came chasing out here?’

‘You know why,’ she returned testily.

‘I know you say you want to take Serine home, but for pity’s sake, why? There has to be some good reason.’

‘Because I don’t like to see her ruining her life!’ she flashed. ‘Serine left me a note saying she’d gone away with some man, some *stranger!* Do you really think I’d sit back and let her get on with it? I know nothing about you, Mr Deville. I had a hell of a job tracing you, and I’m damned if I’m going home before I’ve accomplished what I set out to do!’

‘The choice,’ he said, his arms folded across his powerful chest, ‘is Serine’s. And I think she’s already made that decision.’

‘No, it’s not,’ cried Talia. ‘Tell me, Mr Deville, do you make a habit of living with girls young enough to be your daughter?’

A harsh frown jagged his brow. 'I beg your pardon?'

'How old are you?' she demanded.

'Thirty-six.'

'And Serine's eighteen, just. I think it stinks!'

His eyes narrowed. 'Serine told me she was twenty-three.'

'She would do.'

'Why?'

'Because,' said Talia with exaggerated patience, 'Serine has set her sights on you. She's always fancied marrying a rich man. She must have thought her ship had come in when you asked her to come away with you.'

He shook his head in exasperation. 'Marriage between us has never been mentioned. Serine is going to work for me, that's all.'

'Doing what?' Talia demanded coldly.

'Interior designing.'

'Interior designing?' she questioned with a frown. 'I don't believe this. She's only just finished her college course, she's had absolutely no experience.' Although she had to admit her sister had a natural flair for this sort of thing. But for her actually to con Dervan into employing her was something Talia found difficult to accept.

'I don't think experience matters,' he said. 'She's well able to do the job.'

Talia tossed her head impatiently. 'And in order to do it she has to live here with you? Really, Mr Deville, what do you take me for, a complete idiot?'

'Serine does not live here,' he informed her tersely. 'She has her own apartment.'

For a second Talia did not know what to say. He had virtually knocked the floor from under her feet. But quickly she recovered. 'Then what is she doing here now, in a dress I've never seen before?'

'I'm taking her out for a meal.'

'In which case you'd go to pick her up,' claimed Talia triumphantly.

'I did pick her up, but I forgot my wallet and came back. If you'd been a few minutes later you'd have missed us.'

Talia did not believe a word. There was far more going on between him and Serine than he was admitting; she only had to look at her sister to see it in her eyes. 'You can say what you like, Mr Deville; I still want to take Serine home. Apart from anything else, the house isn't the same without her.'

He frowned. 'Serine lives with you?'

'Of course she does.' And then, suspiciously, 'What did she tell you?'

'That she had her own flat and no commitments.' His black eyes were watchful, never leaving her face for one moment. 'And certainly not that she had a domineering older sister.'

Talia jutted her chin. 'I've brought her up ever since our parents died nine years ago. And it's not been easy.'

'Then perhaps it's time you relinquished your hold, Miss Winslow. The fact that she accepted my job offer proves that she wants to strike out on her own.'

'Are you sticking up for her?' demanded Talia angrily.

'I don't condone her telling me lies, but I can see why she broke away.'

'You're saying I'm too possessive?' Talia's grey eyes flashed hostilely, and two high spots of colour flamed her cheeks.

'Yes, I think you are, and I don't think there's anything else to discuss.'

He crossed the room and opened the door, and Talia was given no chance to defend herself. Serine was standing outside and had obviously been listening to all that was said.

Dervan stood back for her to enter, and the younger girl looked aggressively at Talia, then cautiously at Dervan Deville.

'Why did you lie to me about your age, Serine?' he asked, eyeing her steadily.

She glanced at Talia and without even the grace to look ashamed said, 'I'm sorry, but I really wanted this job, and I knew I looked older. Actually I can't see what age has to do with it.'

'It has nothing,' he admitted, 'but I don't like liars. You didn't tell me you lived with your sister either. You gave me to understand that you had no commitments.'

Serine lowered her eyes demurely. 'I'm sorry, Dervan.'

Talia felt nauseated. Her sister rarely ate humble pie, not unless she wanted to get her own way.

'And so you should be,' he said, but he didn't look unduly annoyed. 'I think you and I have a lot of talking to do. And I also think,' he went on, directing his attention towards Talia, 'that it would be a good idea if you left now.'

'Not before I've spoken to Serine,' she snapped.

'I don't want to speak to her,' said Serine at once.

Dervan nodded. 'No good will be gained by pressing the issue now.'

'Very well,' agreed Talia reluctantly. 'I'll go, but not until you've given me my sister's address. I'll talk to her tomorrow.'

Despite Serine's pleading with him not to, Dervan jotted it down on a slip of paper, silently handing it to Talia. Then, with his hand in the small of her back, he propelled her from the room.

When the front door closed behind her Talia was absolutely fuming. She was doing him a favour, for goodness' sake! Why the hell was he sending her away? But she did not have to find an answer to her question; she already knew it. He had been lying when he said there was nothing between him and Serine. They were having an affair and he wasn't ready yet to relinquish his hold on her. It was as clear as the nose on her face. Even now they were probably in each other's arms, laughing behind her back.

But he would tire of her, and when he did Serine would wonder what had hit her. She was in for a shock. On the other hand, Serine was expert at getting her own way. From an early age she had discovered that she had only to flash her wide green eyes and pout her pretty lips and her father would give her anything she wanted. As she got older she found that it worked with almost any member of the opposite sex, and she used it to her full advantage.

She was never deliberately naughty or disobedient, but she was thoughtless, staying out until all hours, bringing friends home to stay the night without even asking, and rarely tidying her room. Talia washed her clothes and cooked her meals and cleaned the house, and there was never a word of thanks. Serine was purely interested in having a good time. 'You enjoy doing it,' she would say whenever Talia grumbled.

There was a hotel close by and Talia went into it, crossing to the reception desk. 'I'd like to book a single room for tonight,' she said firmly.

The girl pulled a rueful face. 'I'm sorry, we're fully booked.'

'But surely you have something—anything. Just for tonight?'

'I'm afraid not,' apologised the girl again.

Talia turned away, disappointed, and it took her over an hour to find an apartment. Her feet ached and her head ached and she was in an even blacker mood. A shower refreshed her, but did nothing for her temper.

She changed into the cotton skirt and blouse she had brought with her; there had seemed no point in packing more when she intended taking Serine straight home. She ought to have known it would not be that easy.

Afterwards she took a stroll through the palm-lined streets. There were single or two-storied apartments on either side, painted in traditional Lanzarotean colours of green and white, with pleasant gardens alive with colour.

It began to grow dark, and Talia realised she was hungry. She'd hardly touched her meal on the plane and had only nibbled a slice of toast before leaving home. The apartments gave way to shops and discos and restaurants, the pavement thronged with holidaymakers all intent on enjoying themselves.

She met the couple who had been her companions on the plane and they insisted she join them. But Talia found it difficult to concentrate on conversation when Serine and Dervan Deville were so much in her mind, and as soon as she had finished eating she excused herself.

The next morning she woke early to the sound of laughter and shouting in the pool outside her window, and she would have loved a swim, except that she had no swimsuit. Instead she decided to go and tackle Serine before she left for work.

But when she got to the address Dervan had given her she discovered that Serine had already left. There was nothing for it then, thought Talia, but to go to the office. She had no intention of waiting all day.

It was nothing more than a huge purpose-built cabin overlooking a building site which sloped down to the seashore, and it was easy to see that when the apartment homes were built they would command superb views.

Serine saw Talia coming and met her at the door. She was furious. 'Why can't you leave me alone?' she demanded. 'For the first time I thought I'd be able to lead my own life without you interfering. Just go!'

'Not unless you come with me,' said Talia firmly.

Serine's chin jutted. 'I am not coming, Talia. Haven't I made myself clear?' She was wearing a straight grey skirt this morning, with a demure white blouse, but it added to rather than detracted from her sensuality, and it was easy to see why Dervan was interested.

Talia's skin crawled at the thought of this experienced man, this man of the world, touching her baby sister. It was positively indecent! She could not think of Serine as a grown-up person in her own right, well able to look after herself and have adult relationships if she so wanted.

'Serine, please,' she said persuasively, 'can't you see that you're making a fool of yourself? Dervan Deville's not interested in you. He's playing around.'

Serine turned and went inside, Talia following. 'Do you know what I think?' demanded the younger girl. 'I think you're jealous. You've never had a steady boyfriend and you hate the thought of me—'

'Oh, Serine, it's not that, you know it isn't.' Talia tried to take her sister into her arms.

But Serine pushed her away. 'I can't think of any other reason why you're trying to split me and Dervan up.'

Talia shook her head sadly. 'He's using you, Serine. The job's just a front. You'll never get anywhere with him.'

'That's where you're mistaken,' said Serine. 'He's very fond of me.'

‘But he doesn’t love you, and he’ll never marry you, if that’s what you’ve got in mind.’

‘He will, in time,’ responded Serine confidently. ‘We get on well together, and he’s a marvellous architect. He has the most brilliant mind ever. He’s worked all over the world.’

And this was what attracted Serine. She was in love with his glamorous image, nothing more.

‘Money doesn’t buy happiness,’ said Talia gently.

‘Nor does poverty,’ retorted Serine. ‘The trouble with you is you have no ambition. You sit at home all day typing your pathetic letters and reports, you never go out, you never see anyone. I want more from life than that, and I mean to have it.’

‘You won’t get it with Mr Deville.’ Talia ignored her sister’s outburst. Serine never had appreciated that the work she did at home was in order to earn enough money to keep the two of them. And typing all day and doing the housework in the evenings and weekends left her precious little time for relationships. 'Not now he knows what game you're playing.'

Serine glanced at her haughtily. 'It might surprise you to know that your coming here hasn't made the slightest bit of difference.'

'Then Dervan Deville's a fool, and I shall tell him so.'

'Go ahead.'

Talia whirled at the male voice from behind, her heartbeats quickening slightly, but she lifted her chin and held his gaze. 'If you intend carrying on your affair with my sister despite what I've told you, then you are indeed a fool, Mr Deville.'

'You're still of that opinion?' He wore fawn lightweight trousers and a cream shirt, and his tan looked deeper than it had yesterday. He had a powerful physique and a personality to match, but Talia refused to let him intimidate her.

'Of course. But I didn't come here to speak with you, Mr Deville.'

'I never for one moment thought you had. But I did think you'd wait until this evening to speak with your sister. She has work to do here.'

'And if you thought I was going to sit around all day twiddling my thumbs then you were mistaken,' she informed him tartly.

He turned to the younger girl. 'Serine, I suggest you go to your office. And you,' his eyes rested on Talia, 'had better leave. This is neither the time nor the place for family arguments.'

With a smirk, and with her head held high, Serine disappeared.

'Somehow I think,' said Dervan, 'that all the talking in the world will make no difference to Serine. And I'm definitely not going to persuade her to come home with you. She has some marvellous design ideas. She's definitely going to be an asset to my company. I should hate to have to begin my search all over again. And personally,' he went on after a slight pause, 'I think you're too much of an interfering busybody. For pity's sake leave your sister alone.'

Talia gasped at his nerve. 'I happen to love my sister, Mr Deville, and I'm concerned for her. More especially since I've met you. There's no way that I'm going to leave this island without her.'

He was unmoved by her outburst 'Serine's very adamant. We had a good long talk about it last night.'

Talia eyed him contemptuously. 'You have a lot to learn about my sister, Mr Deville.'

He smiled. 'I've already learned a lot.'

Talia bet he had, and the thought of his intimacy with Serine appalled her. But it suddenly struck her that if anyone could change Serine's mind it would be Dervan. If she told him the whole story then he would understand, and he would help her persuade Serine to go home.

She also knew it was no use talking to him while Serine was anywhere near, she needed to get him on his own. Which would be difficult, as they seemed to spend most of their time together. She eyed him aggressively. 'I can see I'm not going to get anywhere this morning, but don't think I'm leaving yet.' She raised her voice, 'I'll see you later, Serine,' and walked out of the office.

A few yards away from the site was a pavement café, and Talia ordered coffee and prepared to wait. The sun was hot on her head and shoulders and she thought of the cold damp November weather she had left behind in England. In one way Serine was lucky. This was a perfect place to spend a few months. If only her reasons for being here were better ones!

Talia's patience was rewarded two hours later when Dervan came out of his office. She stood up and approached him as he walked towards a blue Mercedes. When he saw her he frowned with annoyance.

'Really, Miss Winslow, do you realise you're making an absolute nuisance of yourself? What is it now?'

'I think you and I should talk.'

His black brows drew together. 'I think we've talked enough.' He turned the key in the lock and opened the door.

'It's very important that you should know the whole story,' she said determinedly.

He rested one elbow on the top of the door and stared at her coldly. 'I have no intention of getting involved in family disputes.'

'Not when you're the cause of it?' she demanded, her whole body bristling with indignation.

His eyes narrowed. 'All I did was offer Serine a job. I didn't ask for any of this.'

'But you've got it!' she spat. 'You're involved whether you want to be or not and I want to talk to you.'

'Very well,' he said without enthusiasm, 'but not now.' He glanced at the slim gold watch on his wrist. 'In fact if I don't hurry

I shall be late for my appointment. I'll see you this evening. Where are you staying?'

Talia gave him the address of the apartment complex, and he nodded. 'I'll be there at seven.' And without another word he got into his car and drove away.

She stared after Dervan until he disappeared from sight and then glanced across at his site office, wondering whether it was worth paying her sister another visit. They'd had no chance at all to speak privately. Didn't Serine know how much she was upsetting her by behaving like this? On the other hand, it might make matters worse. Far better to wait until this evening when she might be able to get Dervan Deville on her side.

As it was obvious she would be spending yet another night here, Talia went back to her apartment and rinsed out the bra and pants she had worn the previous day, draping them over the clothes airer that was provided by the complex.

What now? Something to eat perhaps?

She ordered sandwiches in the bar and chatted to one or two of the holidaymakers, then she returned to her apartment and lay down to rest. Surprisingly, she slept and when she awoke she took another shower and prepared herself to wait for Dervan's arrival.

She picked up the in-flight magazine she had popped into her bag when leaving the plane and glanced through the pages. In an advertisement for aftershave the male model looked remarkably like Dervan. He had the same strong face and square jaw, the same straight nose and moulded lips. Only his hair was different. Dervan's was longer and thicker, but the eyes were the same, black and mysterious and sensual. Talia felt a stirring inside her and threw down the magazine.

She went outside, and the pool was empty, the whole area deserted. It was six o'clock, and everyone had gone indoors to get ready for whatever it was they had decided to do this evening. Between the buildings she could see the sun already sinking below the horizon. The sky would soon be blood-red and darkness would fall quickly.

It was beginning to grow chilly, and Talia fetched a cardigan and slipped it around her shoulders. She went for a walk which lasted half an hour and took her to the beach and back. The sea was calm and smooth and there were none of those winds which she had been told whistled across the island.

Time went by on leaden feet, and at a minute to seven Dervan arrived. He had not yet changed and he looked tired. Talia wondered whether to ask him inside or suggest they go to a bar somewhere, but he solved her problem by saying, 'Let's sit down—I'm shattered! I've had meetings all day and none of them has gone the way I wanted them to.'

Which did not augur well for what she had to say, thought Talia despondently. She had entertained high hopes for tonight.

'Would you like a cup of coffee?' she asked. 'I'm afraid I haven't anything else.'

He nodded and relaxed into one of the green and yellow cushioned armchairs, resting his head on the back, stretching out his long legs, and closing his eyes.

Talia filled the kettle and reached out two cups. The tiny kitchenette was in a corner of the living-room, so while she waited for the water to boil she leaned back against the sink unit and observed him. He really was like that man in the advertisement.

Slowly his eyes opened, and it was too late for her to look away. 'I'm glad you find me interesting,' he said, his mouth twisted wryly. 'Because you intrigue me too. Would you believe it if I told you that I've been looking forward to this meeting all day?'

CHAPTER TWO

Talia could not imagine why she intrigued Dervan, and she wished with all her heart that he had not caught her looking at him. She did not want him to get the wrong idea.

She turned back to the kettle and proceeded to make the coffee. 'As a matter of fact,' she said carefully, 'I too have been looking forward to this evening. How do you like your coffee?'

'Black no sugar,' he answered at once.

'I want you to know everything about Serine,' she went on. 'Then you'll realise that she's not the girl you think she is and it will be best if she goes home.'

The drinks made, she placed one cup in front of him on the low pine table and her own at the other end. She sat on the edge of the opposite armchair, her knees and ankles together, her hands resting in her lap.

He looked at her intently. 'I'd rather find out about you. I find it absolutely amazing that you're running around after a girl who gives every appearance of being well able to look after herself.'

'I'm not saying she isn't,' replied Talia. 'I'm just trying to stop her making a mistake. As I said to you yesterday, she wants to marry you.'

'I appreciate the warning,' he said with some amusement, 'but I think I can handle my own affairs. The girl I marry—if I ever do get married—will most definitely be in love with me. Nevertheless, I find your sister good company and I don't see why I should stop taking her out. You're worrying for nothing, Talia. Why don't you go home and let Serine get on with her own life? She's a big girl now, too old to have her sister wet-nursing her.'

Talia flashed her eyes angrily. 'You don't

know what you're talking about. I'm not here to protect Serine from herself, I'm here to protect her from you.'

'If you knew me better you wouldn't say that,' he crisped, putting his coffee-cup down on the table so hard that it slopped into the saucer.

'I don't think I want to get to know you any better,' she returned. 'It's easy to see the type of man you are. No man with any conscience would whisk a girl of Serine's age off to the Canary Islands without checking with her family first.'

'I think you're forgetting,' he said tightly, 'that I thought Serine was twenty-three. Had I known her real age and circumstances I would never have allowed her to come here without telling you.'

Talia eyed him aggressively. 'Somehow I don't believe you.'

He shrugged. 'Believe what you like, it's the truth. Perhaps we ought to get down to the real purpose of this talk, though what it is you want to tell me about your sister, I can't imagine. I already know your parents are dead and that you've brought her up—and still feel that you've got to play guardian. What more is there to say?'

It took Talia several seconds to control herself sufficiently to speak without lashing out at him. Did he always have to be so condemning? She picked up her cup and cradled it in her hands, needing something to hold, something to take her tension. 'Serine was only nine when Mum and Dad died. My father had just got his pilot's licence and he took my mother up on his first flight. They crashed in a field not far from where we live—no one ever found out why.'

Dervan looked suitably compassionate. 'I'm sorry, I didn't know that. It must have been terrible for you.'

Talia nodded. 'I was nineteen and in my first job after leaving secretarial college. I tried to look after the home and Serine, but in the end I had to give up my job. Serine was a very wayward child. She'd been thoroughly spoiled and more often than not got her own way. You see, after I was born my mother thought she could have no more children. When Serine came along they were over the moon, and she was petted and pampered and allowed her own way—well, you can see what she's ended up like.'

'I only have your word for that,' said Dervan. 'I've never found her anything other than a good worker and good company.'

'But you saw how she reacted when I turned up. And you know the lies she's told. Surely you don't condone them?'

'No, of course not but she had a very good reason, as it happens.'

'Yes,' snapped Talia, 'because she'd found herself a rich man.'

'I don't think it was that,' said Dervan. 'She was really excited about the job. And I must admit she's showing every sign of being extremely good at it.'

'But she wouldn't be if I hadn't done

typing at home to help put her through college, and to pay for the clothes she always wanted,' retorted Talia sharply. 'Serine has no idea how much I've given up for her sake.'

'And now you resent it, do you?'

'No!' she frowned at once. 'Of course not. But I do wish she'd consulted me before chasing half-way around the world. It was the least she could have done.'

'I think,' said Dervan, eyeing her steadily, 'that it's you who's making the mistake. I think you ought to stop interfering.'

'How can I sit back and let her ruin her life?' she flashed.

'Are you implying that she's ruining her life because of me?' he asked shortly.

'You or any man,' she returned.

'People learn by their mistakes, Talia. You've protected her for too long. It's time you let go and started thinking about yourself. How old are you now, twenty-eight?'

She nodded.

'And how many boyfriends have you had?'

'Not many,' she admitted with a shrug. 'I haven't had time.'

'But Serine's had lots of them, while you've been slaving away keeping the house in order?'

'I suppose so. But she's far prettier than me anyway, and she has a better figure. I—'

'Talia,' he said firmly, 'don't put yourself down. You're a very attractive woman. If I weren't so tired I'd suggest taking you out to dinner, but I'm afraid I wouldn't be very good company tonight.'

Talia could not believe what she had heard. She eyed him in disgust. 'Do you invite out every girl you meet?' How right she had been to worry about her sister! He was nothing but a womaniser.

An eyebrow lifted. 'Only the ones who interest me. She has to have something special.'

'So what's special about me?' she demanded. 'Or is it just to prove to my sister that *she* has no claim on you? Is that what you're trying to do?'

She thought he might be angry with her for being so blunt, but instead he laughed. 'Talia, believe me, this has nothing to do with Serine. Tomorrow night, perhaps? Will that suit you?'

A tremor of awareness ran through her, tightening the back of her throat, quickening her heartbeats. She had felt the same sensation when she looked at the magazine advertisement, only it was much stronger now. Damn it, she did not want to be interested in this man! 'I'm sorry, no.'

'You have other plans?' he frowned.

'No, but if I can persuade Serine to come with me I shall go home tomorrow.'

'And if you can't?'

Talia shrugged. 'Then I shall have to stay until she comes to her senses.'

'Can you afford to?'

'Not really,' she admitted, 'and there's my typing contracts to be considered, but I'm definitely not leaving Serine in your clutches.'

His mouth, which had relaxed over the last few minutes, tightened again. 'You're pretty free with your insults, Talia.'

'I speak the truth as I see it,' she defended.

'And you're determined to stay, and protect your sister from me?'

She nodded. 'For two weeks anyway.' That should give her sufficient time to persuade Serine.

'In that case I have a proposition to make.'

A frown creased Talia's forehead. 'What sort of a proposition?' If it came from this man it had to be devious. She did not trust him one inch.

'You can come and work for me.'

'Work for *you?*' echoed Talia incredulously. 'I wouldn't—'

Dervan held up his hand. 'At least do

me the courtesy of hearing me out.'

Talia lifted her shoulders and looked at him woodenly.

'In that way you will be able to keep an eye on both me and your sister, and you will see there's no foundation at all for your suspicions.'

'I suppose so,' said Talia doubtfully. And the money would definitely be welcome.

'Although,' he went on, 'I still personally think that you're making a big mistake in playing the heavy-handed sister. Serine will always resent you until you give her free rein.'

'Serine can think what she likes,' said Talia. 'What sort of work have you in mind?'

'My secretary needs help—only on a part-time basis, a few hours each morning. And you needn't start for a couple of days, that will give you time to explore the island. It would be criminal to go back without having seen any of it.'

'How very kind of you,' scorned Talia.

'And I think you'd better move out of here and in with your sister.'

Talia's eyes widened. 'She's going to love that! I suppose I'm right in assuming that you're paying for her apartment?'

Dervan inclined his head. 'For the time being, yes.'

'Well, if I'm moving in with her you can stop that. We'll manage it between us.'

His brows rose. 'I'm beginning to see why Serine wanted to get away. You're a very bossy young lady.'

'I don't intend being a kept woman, Mr Deville,' Talia retorted sharply.

The corners of his mouth lifted in amusement. 'Your words, not mine.' When he got no reaction he went on, 'How about clothes—did you bring plenty with you?'

'Of course not,' she snapped. 'I didn't plan on staying.'

'In that case you'd better come to my office first thing in the morning. You can then make whatever phone calls you feel necessary to England, and afterwards we'll go shopping.'

Talia frowned. 'We? *We,* Mr Deville?'

'That's right,' he grinned.

'I'll use your telephone,' she agreed, 'but I'll go shopping by myself, thank you very much.'

'You have enough money?'

'I'll find enough,' she snapped. 'No man's ever bought clothes for me before, and I'm not going to start now.' She had her Visa card, she could use that. She only needed the bare essentials. With a bit of luck, once she was actually living with Serine, she would quickly be able to persuade her to return. As a matter of fact it could work out very well.

'I think you should still allow me to escort you,' he said.

She shook her head. 'It's not necessary.'

'And afterwards I know a great little place where we can have lunch.'

'I said no!' retorted Talia sharply.

In response Dervan pulled her to her

feet and, catching her face firmly between his palms, pressed a kiss to her mouth. He looked deep into her eyes for a long second before stepping back.

Talia felt a shock-wave run through her. His coal-black eyes had sent sensual messages even though his kiss had been carefully platonic, and she could not deny that she felt something.

'Goodbye for now, Talia,' he said softly. 'I'll see you in the morning.' And he had gone before she could speak.

Talia could not believe what had happened. He was so sure of himself. Didn't he ever take no for an answer? But more startling still was her response to his kiss. She dropped into the seat behind her, all thoughts jangled, all senses startlingly alive.

She could suddenly understand and appreciate Serine's interest in Dervan. He stood like a magnet in a field of iron filings. Girls were drawn to him, attracted to him, against their will even.

He had an aura about him that you could see and yet wasn't visible. And Talia knew that the pull of the magnet had already begun.

How long she sat there thinking about him she had no idea, but suddenly Talia realised she was hungry. And yet when she walked to a nearby restaurant and ordered a meal, she found she could eat no more than a few mouthfuls.

There was too much on her mind. Serine. *Dervan.* Whether the house was safe at home. *Dervan.* Two weeks on this island working for Dervan. *Dervan!*

Her thoughts skipped from one to the other, but always came back to the black-haired, black-eyed man whom she had met only yesterday. It felt like a lifetime—well, almost. Certainly much longer than a day.

Talia lay in bed that night a long time before falling asleep. She was appalled by her reaction; she should have felt nothing but loathing for this man who had the gall to try and date her when he was already seeing her sister. But it strengthened her resolve to try and get Serine away from him.

The next morning Talia showered and dressed in the same pink cotton skirt and blouse, drank a cup of coffee and then set out for Dervan's office. She could not help wondering what her sister would say when she found out she was staying, and hoped she wouldn't be too difficult to handle. She hoped Dervan had already told her.

But it was all wishful thinking. Serine scowled when Talia entered the Portakabin. 'What are you doing here again?' she demanded. 'I thought you'd have gone home by now.'

'I'm not going, not without you,' said Talia gently.

Serine frowned. 'You mean you're actually going to stay—here—on the island?'

Talia nodded.

'But you can't—that's not fair! I don't want you to,' pouted Serine.

'I'm afraid it's all arranged,' said Talia, smiling faintly, trying not to antagonise her sister any further. 'And at Dervan's suggestion I'm moving in with you. Didn't he tell you?'

Serine's eyes widened incredulously. 'In with me? When was all this arranged? Why don't I know anything about it?'

'I saw him last night. I—'

'Last night?' questioned Serine harshly. 'But—'

'Serine, please,' interrupted Talia. 'It was my idea. I wanted to tell him about you, about us, our circumstances. I wanted him to realise how immature you really are.' The moment the word was out Talia knew she had said the wrong thing.

'Immature?' blazed Serine. 'I'm eighteen now. I'm an adult—I can do what I like!'

'A date on a calendar makes no difference to a person's state of mind,' said Talia softly. 'You're still exactly the same girl you were a few weeks ago when you were seventeen. It's experience of life that counts, not birthdays.'

'And when am I ever going to get experience if you're on my back all the time?' the younger girl demanded petulantly. 'Why do you think I came out here? I want to be free, free to do what I like and live how I like.'

'Serine, I only want to guide you,' said Talia. 'That's all. Mum and Dad should have been doing this, but since they're gone it's left to me. Please don't resent me. I haven't come here this morning to argue with you.'

Serine's sudden aggression faded and she looked down at her fingers twisting nervously together. 'No, you've come to gloat over the fact that once again you're going to be breathing down my neck.'

'No, I haven't, Serine. I'm here to make a few phone calls. No one at home knows where I am—I don't want people to worry. And after that Dervan's taking me shopping.'

'You don't need Dervan for that,' said Serine crossly.

Dervan smilingly entered the room. 'It was my idea, Serine. Your sister hasn't had time to familiarise herself with the shops, so I thought I'd save her time. Come into my office, Talia, you can make your calls from there.'

Talia followed him, aware of the black looks Serine was throwing her, resigning herself to the fact that there would be another showdown later.

'You look tired,' Dervan observed as he closed the door behind him.

'I didn't sleep well,' she admitted. 'I never do in a strange bed.'

'Sure it's not anything else? Concern for your sister, perhaps?'

'A little, I suppose,' she said. And thinking about him, and the kiss he had given her, though she would never admit that not in a thousand years.

'More than a little, I imagine,' he said drily. 'I heard you and Serine arguing. I wish you'd back off. The girl deserves a break.'

'And what the hell do you think I deserve?' she cried. 'I'd like nothing more than for Serine to meet a nice boy and fall in love and settle down.'

'And until she does you're going to ruin your own life?'

Talia glared. 'It's my duty.'

'You're a fool, Talia. And one day you'll realise it. You'd better get on with your calls.' He turned at the door and gave her the code for England. 'If you have any problems just give me a shout.'

But Talia had no difficulties, and as soon as she had finished she joined Serine and Dervan.

'All done?' he asked

She nodded. 'Yes, thank you.'

'Then we'll go.' And to Serine, 'I'll be back after lunch.'

'After *lunch?*' she ejaculated.

'That's right,' he smiled, and without any further word of explanation he took

Talia's elbow and led her from the office.

'I said I wasn't going to have lunch with you,' she said fiercely once they were alone.

'You don't have any choice,' he said, smiling disarmingly. 'Once I make my mind up to do something I usually do it. You'd best remember that, Talia.'

In his car she found his magnetism so strong that it almost frightened her. She had felt a little bit of it last night, but now it came across in waves of gigantic proportions. She was going to have the greatest difficulty in stopping herself going the same way as her sister.

He wore grey trousers this morning, the fine material moulding itself to his outstretched legs. The musky smell of his aftershave assailed her nostrils, and Talia wondered whether it was the one in the advertisement. She smiled at her own idiocy. That would be too much of a coincidence.

Dervan saw the smile and an eyebrow

rose. 'May I share the joke?'

'It's nothing. My thoughts—silly thoughts.' And he would think her stupid if she told him. Besides, it would give away the fact that she had been thinking about him. She must stop herself doing that, it was dangerous. 'Where are you taking me?'

'Puerto del Carmen—it's easier to park there than Arrecife, and there's a Parigi shop and a Benetton.'

'Hey, wait a minute!' exclaimed Talia. 'I only want something cheap to tide me over the next couple of weeks.'

'False economy,' he said. 'You'll obviously wear whatever you buy afterwards. But there are boutiques as well. You'll have plenty of choice.'

It was a few minutes' ride along the flat coastal road. Inland were folds of brown volcanic mountains, bare of trees but somehow lovely. This island had a unique beauty, and Talia was determined to see more of it before she began working for Dervan. She would hire a car tomorrow and explore as much as she could. It was too good an opportunity to waste.

Dervan went into every shop with her, voicing his opinion, knowing what he would like to see her in, surprising Talia by his unerring good taste. And more surprising still was the fact that she did not after her initial embarrassment resent his opinions. She could not ignore the warmth that stirred her veins, and more than once found herself seeking his approval.

Until she suddenly remembered the green dress Serine had worn the other night. Had Dervan taken her shopping too? Had he eyed her sister up and down as he was her? Talia felt sickened at the thought. And when it came to buying underclothes she forbade him to set foot inside the door.

'I've no intention of asking you to model them in front of me,' he said, frowning at the sudden change in her.

'You're not even going to see them,' snapped Talia. 'Is this how you get your kicks, taking every girl you meet out shopping so that you can lust over her?'

'Every girl?' he asked, his brows knitting together. 'What is this? What are you talking about?'

'I'm thinking specifically about my sister,' said Talia coldly, 'and that green dress she was poured into the night I arrived. Did you choose it for her? And did you ogle her the way you have me? And what else have you bought her?' She was shaking in her anger, completely oblivious to the people who had stopped to listen.

'For pity's sake, Talia, control yourself!' He took her by the shoulders and held her firmly. 'No, I did not take Serine shopping, but yes, I did pay for the dress. It was her choice, and hers alone.'

Talia eyed him coldly and suddenly became aware of the onlookers. 'Let me go!' She twisted away from him and ran into the shop, closing the door behind her. The assistants inside had either missed what was going on or were carefully polite.

Whatever, Talia was able to complete her purchases in relative calm.

They made their way back to his car in silence. Now that Talia had had time to cool down she regretted her outburst. It had been childish and petty, more suited to Serine than herself. 'I think I'd prefer to go back to my apartment,' she said.

Dervan made no comment but nor did he do as she asked. He drove inland, and they were soon in among the mountains. Talia had known it was a volcanic island, but nothing had prepared her for its stark beauty. It was like a lunar landscape, pockmarked and rugged. There were no trees, apart from the odd palm, and only the occasional patches of green where recent rains had encouraged vegetation.

'You either love or hate Lanzarote,' Dervan said when she plucked up the courage to break the silence and comment on the lunar-like landscape. 'Some people say it's ugly and barren, but personally I find it all rather beautiful.'

Talia assumed he saw it with his architect's eye, and she could actually see the anger draining out of him as the lines and shapes communicated something to him.

'But you haven't seen anything yet,' he went on. 'Timanfaya, or Fire Mountain as it's called, is the best region to explore if you're after stark beauty. Two hundred square kilometres of black volcanic mountains and petrified lava.'

'Are the volcanoes still active?' asked Talia with a faint frown.

'The last eruption was well over a hundred years ago,' he told her re-assuringly, 'but previously, in 1730, the eruptions lasted six whole years and destroyed a third of the island—villages, people, the lot.'

Talia gasped. The horror of it did not bear thinking about.

'There are still parts where nothing lives. You really should see it.'

Talia nodded. 'I was thinking of hiring

a car tomorrow. I might go then.'

'I could take you,' he suggested hopefully. 'It's no fun exploring on your own. You'll be so busy looking at your map that you'll miss all the best things.'

'No, thanks,' gritted Talia through her teeth. It was a tempting offer, but she had to remember the type of man he was. Unfortunately nothing seemed to dispel the sheer magnitude of his sensuality.

A muscle jerked in his jaw, but he said no more. He turned on the cassette player instead and the sounds of Sibelius's *Finlandia* filled the car. It was not a piece of music that particularly appealed to Talia, but she had heard it often when her father was alive. He had always said the music soothed him. Talia had never been able to understand that—and it did nothing for her now except bring back memories.

'You look sad,' remarked Dervan after a moment or two. 'I think I made a mistake. I'll take you back.'

Talia shook her head. 'It's this music—it was one of my father's favourite pieces.'

'I'm sorry. Shall I stop it?'

'No, it doesn't matter,' she said at once.

But he stopped it anyway. 'It's a pity your parents died when Serine was so young,' he said. 'It put too much of a burden on you.'

'I've managed.' she said.

'But at what cost? Your own happiness?'

'I've not been unhappy.'

'Serine's lucky she had a sister who was prepared to give up everything to look after her. But now I think that time should come to an end. You've done all you can, Talia.'

'No, I haven't,' she replied sharply, wishing he wouldn't keep on about it. He never lost an opportunity to make his point. 'I shan't be happy until I get her home to England.'

'Even if you do manage to persuade her—which I hope you don't, she's very useful to me,' he added, 'there'll still be some other man you'll worry about. For pity's sake let go of her.'

'Does a mother ever stop worrying about her offspring? I feel the same, totally responsible.'

Dervan shook his head in exasperation. 'Really, Talia, it's not necessary. She's a remarkably independent girl.'

'Independent, stubborn, wayward, wilful, call it what you like. She has a mind of her own and—'

'The more you try to rule her the further away from you she'll grow. I think you're the one who needs to do the growing up, Talia. This is a ridiculous state of affairs.'

'Thank you, Mr Deville,' she said coldly. 'I try my hardest and all I end up with is abuse.'

'There's nothing wrong with Serine,' he said. 'Until you turned up I didn't even realise there was a problem. If you'd just leave her alone.'

Talia rubbed a hand round the back of her neck. 'Go to hell!'

'And the best part about it,' he continued, as though she hadn't spoken, 'is that Serine and I actually complement one another. Her ideas for interior design go absolutely hand in glove with my ideas for buildings. It's phenomenal in a girl so young. She's beginning to handle the whole thing as though she's had years of experience.'

And what better accolade was there than that? 'Meaning that I'll never get you on my side? You want Serine to remain here at whatever cost?'

He shrugged. 'But of course.'

'Then I'm wasting my time. I don't even see the point in my staying to help you.'

Dervan shrugged. 'That's your prerogative. I need help, and I could do with an English girl. Maria's English is good, but there are some things she has difficulty with.'

Talia knew she wouldn't leave the island,

not yet. She still hadn't had a really good chance to speak with her sister. Once they were living together it would be easy. 'I'll stay,' she said, 'but only because of Serine.'

'Of course,' he replied drily.

Suddenly he stopped the car and they were in the centre of a tiny remote village. 'We're eating here?' she asked in surprise. There was no sign of a restaurant.

He nodded. 'In the bar-cum-café where the locals eat. The food's superb. I don't think you'll have any complaints.'

'How did you find it?' she asked.

'Easy,' he shrugged. 'Whenever I'm working abroad I always chat to the locals to find out the best eating places. The tourist spots are invariably a rip-off.'

There was no frontage to the building, The door opened straight on to the street but through the bar and out the other side was a paved area with white iron tables and chairs, gaily covered with red-checked cloths.

'Why, this is lovely!' Talia exclaimed.

Dervan looked pleased by her enthusiasm.

It was early and there were no other diners, but despite the hour Talia was starving. Having eaten very little for two days, she was determined to make up.

They sipped wine while deciding what to order—raw local wine that left a strange taste in Talia's mouth—but it was easy to get used to and she was soon holding out her glass for more. And they nibbled marinated olives and pickled cauliflower while waiting for their food, Talia refusing baby eels or pigs' trotters in garlic sauce. *Tapas,* Dervan called them, these tasty bits of food. 'If you're not careful you can fill yourself up on the stuff,' he warned.

It was very pleasant sitting in the dappled shade of a palm tree. A scrawny grey cat rubbed itself round her ankles, and Talia bent to stroke it. When she lifted her head she met Dervan's eyes close to hers. He too had been watching the cat, or was it her?

There was an instant of mutual attraction, a fraction of a second when they both realised that something was happening to them, or had indeed happened. A spark that shot between them like an electric current. There was no escaping it.

Talia made herself sit back in her seat as if nothing was wrong. 'Tell me about your work,' she invited. Not that she really wanted to discuss his work. She wanted to ponder over this sexual awareness she was feeling, explore the reason why.

'My work, yes,' and she could tell by his tone and his expression that he did not want to talk about it either. His eyes locked into hers and he would not look away. 'I'm afraid it's all rather humdrum, but—'

'Humdrum, nothing!' exclaimed Talia. 'How can designing a holiday complex be humdrum?'

'Actually, it's very exciting.' His smile was wide, his teeth very white. 'And I'm not only doing the designing, I'm developing and financing the whole project.'

Talia's eyes widened. 'I had no idea. I'm impressed.'

'As well you should be. It's going to be a very impressive place—designed exclusively for up-market clients. It will want for nothing.'

Their meal arrived and they continued to talk while they ate, but all the time Talia felt threads of awareness run through her veins, and more than once she had to ask what he said because instead of concentrating on his words she had been thinking what it would be like to be made love to by him. Her mind had never before drifted away like this on a tack of its own, especially such an erotic one. She hoped he would not guess the reason for her preoccupation.

'This fish is excellent, don't you think?' he asked.

Talia nodded and took another forkful, but she could well have been eating fish fingers instead of sea bass. Despite her appetite, she tasted very little of what she ate.

And Dervan too paid her far more attention than he did his food. He watched her constantly, studying in turn her wide-spaced grey eyes, her mouth as she forked food into it, the swell of her breasts beneath the cotton blouse, and she could feel the responding arousal in her body.

Once he stroked her nose with a gentle finger. 'I've never been out with a girl who had freckles. They're beautiful.'

Up until that moment Talia had always hated them. Now she felt differently. The sunshine this last couple of days had brought them out in their hundreds, and she wrinkled her nose delightedly at him. 'Thank you. No one's said that to me before.'

She was sorry when they finished their meal and it was time to leave. On the other hand, perhaps it was as well. Whatever was growing between them, it was happening too quickly and too soon.

Dervan took her hand as they walked out to the car, making sure she was seated comfortably before going round to his own side and unlocking the door.

Inside Talia's feelings were heightened even more. They were in their own little cocoon once again, and she could smell him and breathe him and she wanted to touch him—badly. But although one half of her was thrilled by these new and exciting emotions, the other half was angry because she had come out here hating this man and was now in danger of falling for his undoubted charm.

'I'll take you back to your apartment,' he said, 'and then tonight I'll come and collect you again and move you in with Serine.'

Talia nodded. 'Thank you.'

He drove hard and fast, and when they got there he reached out an armful of parcels and followed her inside. Dumping them on the settee, he turned and took her into his arms. 'Talia, I'm sorry, but I have to do this.' His mouth on hers dispelled every sensible thought in her head. She was aware of moaning softly as her lips parted and she pressed her body close to the long, hard maleness of his. For a few seconds time had no meaning.

Then abruptly it was over. He pulled away and held her at arm's length. 'Will you let me take you to Timanfaya tomorrow?' he asked softly.

Talia shook her head. He had charm, he had sex-appeal, he had charisma, he had everything any girl could ever want, and yet she had to say no. She was here to prise Serine away from him, not become a victim herself. She deliberately made her tone hard. 'No, Dervan, I have no intention of becoming another statistic.'

He frowned, a quick frown of surprise, then his mouth firmed. 'I see. I obviously got the wrong impression. I'm sorry.' And he walked out of the apartment.

CHAPTER THREE

Talia had no regrets about telling Dervan that she did not want to go out with him. From that moment in the café there had been a mutual attraction, and his kiss had done things to her that should never be allowed, but he'd had exactly the same effect on her sister, and probably other girls as well. He gave them his all while he was with them and then turned his attention on someone else the moment their backs were turned. He was a swine!

Talia yanked off her clothes and stood beneath the shower, but as her hands soaped her body she imagined it was Dervan touching her, Dervan caressing her, Dervan feeling every contour and curve, and she grew angry at her own foolishness. Heavens, weren't these the sort of fantasies dreamed up by impressionable teenagers? Serine, for instance?

At the thought of her sister she sobered. Had Serine had these same notions? Had she in fact actually shared a shower with Dervan and enjoyed the eroticism of his naked body against hers? Admittedly he said he hadn't bedded her, and she believed him, but he had undoubtedly shared certain intimacies. The thought stuck in Talia's throat like a fish-bone, and she savagely turned off the tap. Wrapping herself sarong-wise in a towel, she threw herself on to the bed.

She was insane to even let the briefest flicker of desire touch her. Besides, if Dervan had reached the age of thirty-six without getting married it proved he was not the settling-down type. Getting involved with him would be sheer madness. Serine herself was heading for disaster, even though she couldn't yet see it. Damn the man. *Damn him!*

Shooting to her feet again, Talia rummaged through the parcels and pulled out her new bikini. A vigorous swim would rid her mind of him.

The bikini was a bronzy-green with bold orange splashes, and she looked like a tropical butterfly as she dived into the pool. Two English boys and a girl were playing with a soft blow-up ball advertising Coca-Cola and they asked her to join them. She spent the next half-hour enjoying a ferocious game of handball.

Eventually they all dropped exhausted on to blue and green striped loungers which fringed the pool. 'That was great,' said the boy, who had introduced himself as Paul. 'Say, Talia, what are you doing tonight? How'd you like to join us? We're going for a pizza and then on to a disco.'

'Oh, yes, do come,' added Karen enthusiastically. 'My brother hates being the odd one out. It'll be perfect.'

Adrian, the third member of the trio,

nodded his approval.

Talia looked at their eager faces and suddenly wished that she was staying on here. She could do with some company other than her sister and Dervan. But she knew she had to keep her eye on Serine, so she shook her head. 'I'm sorry, I'm moving out of here this evening. I'm going to stay with my sister.'

Paul looked disappointed. 'That's a shame.'

'But there's no reason why I can't come out with you some other time,' she added.

'Like tomorrow?' asked Paul eagerly. 'I'll hire a car and we can go wherever you like. Just the two of us.'

Talia frowned.

'It will give Karen and Adrian an opportunity to have some time on their own,' he explained.

A ring on Karen's left hand told Talia that they were engaged, and she thought it admirable that they had brought Paul along with them, so she smiled and nodded. 'OK.' Dervan had been right about exploring on her own. She would have fun with Paul. 'I'll give you my new address and you can pick me up.'

'Good,' grinned Paul, patting the lounger beside him. 'Come and lie here, Talia. Let's leave these two lovebirds to get on with it.'

He was tall and fair with a physique like a weightlifter. He had a permanently cheerful expression, and Talia guessed he was a lot of fun. His sister, too, was blonde, Adrian being the only dark one amongst them. All around she could hear the murmur of conversation, the thrashing of water, an occasional shriek of pure enjoyment, a child crying. She had never envisaged, a few short days ago, that she would be soaking up the sun in the Canary Islands.

Always, or at least since her parents died, Talia had lived her life to a routine. This was something she had not accounted for, but nevertheless she was determined to enjoy every minute while it lasted.

The remainder of the afternoon passed slowly but pleasantly. She told Paul a little bit about Serine, the fact that she was having some sort of relationship with her boss and how worried she was about her.

'I'm sure things will work out,' he said encouragingly.

Gradually the heat went out of the sun and everyone gathered up towels and books, sun-creams and bags, and headed for their bungalow apartments. It was time to get ready for an evening's enjoyment. Talia wondered what sort of an evening she was going to have.

After another shower she pulled on one of her new dresses. It was sleeveless, buttoned all the way down the front, had a tie belt and big patch pockets on the hips. The lovely strong lemon colour suited her. Her shiny chestnut hair fell in deep waves just below her shoulders, and she applied green eyeshadow and a touch of mascara and was in the middle of putting on her lipstick when Dervan arrived.

She hoped he didn't think she was dressing up for his benefit, and suddenly wished she hadn't bothered with make-up. But it was too late now. She opened the door and let him in. He gave her no more than a cursory glance. 'Are you ready?' he asked.

Talia nodded. Her morning's purchases, plus the few bits and pieces she had brought with her, were piled neatly on the settee.

'Then let's go.' His tone was terse. Obviously he was still annoyed with her because she had refused to go out with him.

Mentally shrugging, Talia followed. Paul was walking past as they emerged and he smiled at her cheerfully. 'I'll see you tomorrow.'

Talia nodded. 'OK, Paul.'

Dervan frowned as they climbed into the car. 'Who was that?' he asked.

'Someone I met this afternoon.'

'And you're going out with him, when you wouldn't go with me?' His brow was as black as a thundercloud as he let out the clutch.

'There's a difference,' she defended. 'Paul's here on holiday. I won't feel guilty that I'm keeping him away from anything.'

He crashed the gears and cursed. 'Don't try to make excuses, Talia! The truth of the matter is that you're scared.'

'Of what?' she demanded.

'Me, of course.'

He was so close to the truth that it was alarming, but she raised her fine brows and looked at him boldly. 'If you think that you're an egotistical swine. You're forgetting, I know the type of man you are. You lured my sister into your snare, but I'm hardly likely to follow suit. In case you've forgotten, I'm here to split you and Serine up, not get myself into a similar situation!'

His lips clamped and he clenched the

wheel far more tightly than was necessary. 'Whatever you might think, Talia, I am not in the habit of carrying on with every girl, I meet. I genuinely enjoy your company, and I got the impression yesterday that you enjoyed mine. But don't worry, I shall be careful not to make the same mistake again.'

Talia tried to pretend that his words did not hurt, but deep down inside they did. She had enjoyed his company, very much, and it was for just that reason that she had put a stop to things—before they got out of hand.

Serine's apartment was a few minutes' drive away, and Talia was relieved when he pulled up outside. The complex was very similar to the one she had just left with two-storied apartments fanning out around a pool. Serine opened the door and Dervan carried Talia's things in, then he climbed back into his car and drove away.

Serine watched him go, then closed the

door and turned on Talia. 'How dare you?' she exclaimed.

'How dare I what?' Talia was completely taken aback.

'Have lunch with Dervan.'

Talia frowned. 'It was no big deal and it certainly wasn't my idea.'

'I know what you're trying to do,' claimed Serine. 'You're after Dervan for yourself!'

'No, I'm not. I—'

'Then what are you doing?' Serine paced the length of the room and turned back again. She wore a tight tiger-print dress and her green eyes made her look every inch a jungle cat. 'You could quite easily have said no. What did you do while you were out? What did you tell him?'

'Nothing,' answered Talia. 'Serine, really, I—'

'Nothing, my foot!' Serine broke in yet again. 'He came back to the office and practically ignored me. And when I tried to discuss some of my ideas he told me they were no good and to start all over again.' Tears began to slide down her cheeks, her brief spurt of anger fading. 'I want to know what you said about me!'

'Serine,' said Talia gently, 'we didn't talk about you, really we didn't.'

Serine dropped down on to the settee. 'It's all going wrong,' she choked. 'Before you came he had eyes for no one but me. We were getting on like a house on fire.'

Talia sat too and put her arm about her sister's shoulders. 'Serine, I think you've got the wrong idea about Dervan. He thinks you're a marvel at your job, but it doesn't go any further than that.'

'It does, it does!' Serine protested, raising her tear-stained face. 'He was always taking me out and buying me things. We got on well together.'

'Serine, my darling, don't you realise that you're reading more into it than there is? Besides, he's far too old for you.'

Serine shook her head. 'You're only

saying that because you're attracted to him yourself.'

'Oh, Serine, I'm not.' Talia felt the lie was justified. 'If you must know, he asked me to go out with him tomorrow and I refused.'

'You did?' Hope sprang into Serine's eyes.

'Yes, I did, and it would be best if you didn't go out with him again either.'

'There you go again!' cried Serine, shrugging Talia off and springing to her feet. 'You've never wanted me to have any fun, ever!'

Talia shook her head despairingly. 'Serine, all I've ever wanted is for you to make a success of your life. And you can do that now if you don't make a fool of yourself over Dervan. Perhaps you'd like to tell me which is my room—I'd like to unpack.'

She wished Serine hadn't started this argument; she would have liked time to settle in. She was already tired from her altercation with Dervan.

'You can have that room,' said Serine sulkily, pointing to a door opposite.

Talia picked up her bags and shut herself in. It was a more luxurious room than the one she had left behind, with a proper dressing-table with a lighted mirror, and a good-sized chest of drawers as well as a deep wardrobe.

After putting away her clothes she lay on the bed for a few minutes. But it was no good, she would have to talk to Serine again. They couldn't go on like this. She had to make her sister see that there was no future for her and Dervan.

But when she went back into the living-room Serine was on her way out. Talia frowned. 'Where are you going?' she asked.

'Out.'

'With Dervan?'

Serine shrugged. 'No, as a matter of fact.'

'Then with whom? I've only just got here, Serine. We have to talk. We have to clear this thing up once and for all.'

'That's why I'm going,' said Serine. 'I don't want to talk.'

Talia said no more. There was no point. She would wait until her sister was in a more approachable mood.

It was almost two when Serine finally came home. Talia had lain awake listening and worrying, and only now did she settle down to sleep. But the next morning Serine was in high spirits.

'Good morning, my dear sister,' she smiled as Talia walked out of her bedroom. 'Would you like a cup of coffee?'

Talia's eyes widened in surprise. 'Well, yes, I would, thank you very much. What's happened to you this morning? You're not usually this cheerful first thing.'

'I had a good night,' replied Serine, stretching her arms above her head and smiling her satisfaction. 'A very good night, as a matter of fact.' She wore a short, sheer nightdress and devoid of make-up she looked about sixteen. 'Toast?'

Talia nodded. It was so unusual for Serine to look after her that there had to be something wrong. 'Where did you go?' she asked, deliberately keeping her tone casual.

Serine's smile widened, but she turned her head away from Talia as she answered. 'I met Dervan.'

'But I thought—'

'I know. He just happened to be in the same bar where I went.'

'And you'd no idea he'd be there?' demanded Talia sceptically.

Serine's glance was defensive. 'It's a free country.'

'Oh, Serine!' sighed Talia, but she said no more, because she had made up her mind during the night to stop harassing her sister, for the next few days at least. It might work. She might listen to her if they were friends again.

Serine buttered Talia's toast and pushed it across the table towards her. 'Who's Paul?' she asked.

Talia's eyes widened. 'Someone I met yesterday. Who told you? Dervan?'

Serine nodded. 'He was quite curious about him, as a matter of fact. And so am I,' she smiled, 'so come on, tell me all about him.'

'There's nothing to tell, Serine.' And why had Dervan been asking questions? 'He's just a boy I met at the pool. He's here with his sister and her fiancé. He feels a bit *de trop,* so he asked me out.'

'Is he good-looking?'

Talia shrugged. 'I suppose so. He has a good body, and he's blond and he's lots of fun.'

Serine frowned. 'He doesn't sound like your type. Dervan didn't think so either.'

'He actually said that?' It was Talia's turn to frown. She couldn't believe this. Dervan had been understandably annoyed because she was going out with Paul instead of him, but there was surely no reason for him to ask about the boy, or voice his opinion? Only a jealous man would do that. 'How would he know what my type was?'

'From what I've told him about you,' said Serine. 'Someone serious, who's happy staying in rather than getting out and having a good time. Heavens, is that the time? I must get ready, Dervan will be here shortly.'

Talia frowned. 'Does he always pick you up?'

'Not usually,' answered her sister with a wide smile.

So why today? wondered Talia.

Serine went into the bathroom, Talia nibbled her toast, and the doorbell rang. 'Will you get it?' called Serine.

Talia thanked her lucky stars that her nightdress was a respectable cotton. 'Good morning, Dervan,' she said coolly as she opened the door, trying to ignore the sudden quickening of her pulses.

'Good morning, Talia.' He was wearing a blue lightweight suit today, with a paler blue shirt. His hair was still damp from his shower and consequently curled more than usual. It suited him. He smelled clean and fresh, and his sexuality was even more pronounced.

'Do sit down,' she invited.

'Thank you.' He perched on the edge of one of the chairs at the table, and Talia resumed her own seat.

'Would you like a cup of coffee?'

'No, thanks.'

They were like two strangers, thought Talia, except for the way he was looking at her—there was nothing cool and distant about that. It was as though he was trying to see through her nightdress to her naked body beneath, and her senses stirred, and she wondered whether he had any idea what he was doing to her.

'I was surprised,' she said, 'when my sister said you were picking her up.'

'In other words,' he commented drily, 'you disapprove?'

'As a matter of fact, yes, I do.'

'Why?'

'Isn't it obvious? You told me there was nothing serious between you and Serine, yet you kept her out until two this morning and you're here to pick her up again at eight. If they aren't the actions of a man who can't see enough of a girl, then I don't know what they are.'

'Hasn't it occurred to you that I could be here to see you?'

Talia wished she could believe that but she knew it was not so. 'I doubt it. I made it perfectly clear how I feel.'

Dervan nodded grimly, and at that moment Serine came out of the bathroom wrapped in nothing more than a towel. She gave Dervan a brilliant smile. 'I won't be long,' she told him.

Talia saw him looking at her long, shapely legs and felt sickened. He could deny feeling anything for her sister as much as he liked, she would never believe him. She picked up her cup of coffee and took a sip, cradling it in her hands, looking at Dervan over the brim.

'Is something wrong?' he enquired harshly.

'I was wondering how often you've seen my sister like that. She didn't seem worried by her state of undress, almost as though it were an everyday occurrence.'

His mouth firmed, and a muscle tensed in his jaw. 'You're absolutely determined to think the worst of me, aren't you?'

'You've given me no reason to believe otherwise.'

He snorted angrily and bounced to his feet. 'Really, Talia, at times I could strangle you! You can't see any further than the end of your nose.'

'Maybe not,' she answered, 'but Serine's been walking on cloud nine all morning—so something must have happened between you last night.'

He shook his head despairingly. 'Serine sought me out. I bought her a couple of drinks, that's all.'

'And then took her back to your villa and—'

'Yes, as a matter of fact, Talia, I did take her back,' he cut in brusquely. 'But shall I tell you what we were doing? Discussing some of Serine's design ideas. And if she read anything into that then it has nothing to do with me.'

He sounded as though he were speaking the truth, yet how could she believe him? Serine was definitely on a high this morning.

'What's going on out there? Are you two having an argument?' Serine's voice came from her bedroom and she opened the door, popping her head round to grin at them.

'About you, as a matter of fact,' replied Talia before she could stop herself.

Serine's smile faded, and Dervan said crisply, 'If you're ready we'll go.'

'Give me another couple of minutes,' she answered, and closed the door again.

Silence fell between them. Dervan paced

the room, looking at Talia every few seconds as though expecting her to apologise. But she was damned if she would. 'I think I'll go and get ready too,' she said.

'Ah, yes, you're going out with Paul whatever-his-name-is today, aren't you? But don't make any more arrangements. I want you in the office tomorrow.'

Talia lifted her chin. 'I haven't forgotten.'

He came across and stood close to her, so close that she could feel the heat of his body and her pulses started up all over again, her heart thudding against her ribcage. 'Be careful, Talia,' he warned. 'You know nothing about him.'

'I trust my instincts,' she retorted crisply.

His hands came down on her shoulders and his eyes were very close to hers. 'No matter what you might think of me, Talia, I would never do anything to harm you. Just watch that this boy doesn't either, or I might have to deal with him.'

She looked into the blackness of his eyes

and her whole body set on fire. She very much wanted him to kiss her. But at that moment Serine's bedroom door opened. 'I'm ready, Dervan. I'm sorry ...' She stopped when she saw Dervan holding Talia and frowned. 'What's going on?'

'Nothing,' he answered abruptly, letting go of Talia and turning to the younger girl. 'I was simply warning Talia about Paul.'

'Why should she need warning?' asked Serine.

'Because she's putting herself in his hands before she's had the opportunity to get to know him. It's foolhardiness. Oh, come on, let's go.'

But before he had reached the door the bell rang. When Dervan opened it Paul's cheerful grin did not waver, though his eyes registered an instant of surprise. 'Good morning, is Talia ready?'

Dervan stood back. 'You'd better come in.'

Talia had not been expecting Paul for another hour and again was conscious of the fact that she was not dressed. She smiled weakly. 'Hello, Paul, you're an early bird.'

'I'm sorry if I'm too early. Shall I go and come back again?' He looked at Dervan and Serine and then back at Talia.

'No, don't be silly,' she said. 'I'm just about to get ready—I won't be long. This is my sister, Serine, and this is Mr Deville, her boss.' And to them, 'This is Paul Rogers.'

'Hi, Serine, nice to meet you.' Paul looked the younger girl up and down and was clearly impressed—which did not surprise Talia, because it happened all the time. 'You too, Mr Deville. You're a lucky man.'

Dervan did not ask why; instead he said harshly to Talia, 'If you'd like to go and get ready, we'll keep Paul company.'

Meaning that he didn't trust Paul to keep his hands off her once they were alone. Talia looked at him coldly. 'I don't think that will be necessary, thank you. I won't keep Paul waiting long.'

Their eyes met and clashed for a second, but he didn't press the matter further. 'In that case, we'll go.'

In the doorway Serine looked back over her shoulder. 'Have a good time, you two. You can tell me all about it tonight, Talia.'

Dervan said nothing, the rigidity of his back expressing his mood all too clearly.

'I'm sorry about that,' said Talia, once they were alone. 'It's been all go this morning.'

Paul grinned. 'Don't be sorry, I know I came earlier than I said, but I thought it would give us more time to explore. Your sister's a stunner, isn't she?'

'You're not the only one to think that,' said Talia coolly.

'Oh, crumbs, I apologise.' He caught her hurt immediately. 'I didn't mean she was better than you. You're beautiful too, in a different way. No one would guess you were sisters. I don't blame her boss, though, for having an affair with her.'

'He's not having an affair!' shot Talia. 'I didn't say that. They just go out together sometimes.'

Paul grimaced. 'I really am putting my foot in it, aren't I? Look, you go and get ready and I'll clear away the breakfast things. How does that sound?'

'I can't let you do that,' protested Talia.

'But I will,' he said, 'because then we'll get away more quickly.'

Talia reluctantly agreed, and within fifteen minutes they were ready to go. In the car she asked him why he had come on holiday with his sister. It still seemed strange to her when they were so obviously keen to be alone.

'Karen insisted,' he told her. 'She's a sister in a million. Our parents died in a road accident last year and we've clung to each other ever since.'

Talia nodded sympathetically. 'That

happened to Serine and me. Nine years ago.'

'Then we're orphans together?' he grinned. 'I knew there was a bond between us. I felt it as soon as we met.'

Talia smiled. He could be a charmer when he chose, there was no doubt about it. His jeans and T-shirt were no comparison to Dervan's designer clothes, but they were the standard uniform for his age and they were clean and well pressed.

They headed north, past the airport and the busy capital of Arrecife, looking in wonder about them at all that was new and different and awe-inspiring.

They hardly ever stopped talking. Paul was a mine of information and he had a fund of funny stories. 'Tell me what it's been like for you and Serine,' he said in one of his more serious moments. 'She couldn't have been very old when your parents died. You had an enormous responsibility.'

'She was nine, and I was nineteen. It's

been very difficult, I must admit. I had to give up my job.'

'And now she's fled the nest and you're free again?'

'Something like that,' agreed Talia.

He frowned at her sharp tone. 'It's not all as it seems?'

'Serine hates being poor. That's why she's latched on to Dervan Deville.'

'And you don't approve?'

She shook her head strongly. 'No, I don't. That's why I'm here. He's far too old for her.'

'More suited to you, I would think,' said Paul.

Talia's head jerked. 'Whatever makes you say that?'

'Am I wrong? You do fancy him, don't you? And he was rather protective about you, I thought. He didn't like leaving us together until you were properly dressed.'

Paul was more astute than she had given him credit for, decided Talia. 'I find him attractive,' she answered slowly, wanting to be totally honest, 'but it's madness. Dervan's a wanderer. He travels the world in his work, he's never likely to get married. That's why I think Serine's making a fool of herself. But she won't listen to me.'

'It's a pity there's such an age gap between you,' he said. 'I can understand her resentment. Karen and I were born within thirteen months of each other, that's why we're so close.'

'How old are you?' asked Talia.

'Twenty. Karen's twenty-one.'

Talia's surprise registered on her face. Paul looked and acted much older.

He grinned. 'Our parents always taught us to be independent. I've had quite a tough upbringing, although it was never short of love and consideration. And how I've thanked them for it since.'

'It's a pity Serine couldn't have met someone like you,' she said. 'You'd be good for her. My parents spoiled her unashamedly, and I've had to cope with it. I somehow think you'd be able to put her in her place without her even realising it.'

'I'd like to try,' he nodded, a sort of dreamy look entering his eyes as he thought of Serine. And then, realising what he had said, he pulled himself together. 'I'm sorry, Talia, I've done it again. My father would have rapped my knuckles for being so rude.'

'Don't worry—I'm used to it,' she smiled. 'Serine's always had more boy-friends than me. Besides, I'm too old for you.'

'I enjoy your company very much,' he admitted.

'And I yours.'

'So you will come out with me again?'

She nodded. 'When I can. I'm going to do some part-time work for Dervan.'

His brows rose in surprise.

'It's true. Apparently his secretary needs help, and as I need some money because I'm staying on much longer than I intended, it was too good an offer to turn down.'

Their conversation turned to other subjects, and soon they found a perfect little cove filled with white sand, a delightful surprise after following mile upon mile of dark volcanic rocks and equally black sand. It was as though someone had sprayed the area from a great height—and yet it had to be natural. They spent the whole day swimming and sunbathing and forgot all about exploring the rest of the island.

Paul gave her every minute of his attention, holding an intelligent conversation one moment, making her convulse with laughter the next. Flirting outrageously, then treating her like one of the lads a few seconds later by telling her bawdy jokes. He sensed her mood changes, the moments when she went quiet and her thoughts were far away, and he put himself out to ensure that she had a good time.

'If you like,' he said, when they got

back, 'I'll give you and Serine a lift to work tomorrow.'

'No, Paul,' answered Talia at once. 'I couldn't possibly let you do that.'

'But I'd like to. What time do you go, about eight?'

Talia nodded.

'I'll be here,' he grinned. 'It will ease my conscience for bringing you home early.' He had already explained that he was going out with his sister and her fiancé tonight.

As she walked into the apartment Talia smiled to herself. It was so easy to guess why Paul had offered; he was after an excuse to see Serine again. But when she found a note from her sister saying that she had gone out to dinner with Dervan all her fears came tumbling back. Somehow she had to split the two of them up. She wondered whether Paul was the answer.

CHAPTER FOUR

Talia was already showered and dressed when Serine got up the next morning, and the younger girl eyed her sister in amazement. 'Where are you going, out with Paul again?'

'Hasn't Dervan told you?' asked Talia. 'I'm coming to help out at the office.'

'You're what?' cried Serine, her eyes widening in amazement. 'Whose idea was that? No, don't tell me—it was yours. You're not content with moving in with me, you want to keep your eye on me all day as well!'

Talia groaned inwardly. She realised she ought to have told Serine earlier about the job, but somehow there hadn't been an opportunity. And she really had thought Dervan would mention it. 'Serine,' she said softly, 'it's nothing like that. Dervan said his secretary has too much to do and he asked whether I'd give her a hand. It's only for a couple of weeks—I can't spare any more time.'

Serine still looked suspicious. 'Maria's never mentioned to me that she can't cope.'

'I don't know anything about that,' shrugged Talia. 'All I know is that Dervan asked.'

'But you didn't have to agree. What's going on between you two?'

'Nothing, for heaven's sake!' said Talia strongly.

'Dervan's changed since you came on the scene.' All the fight suddenly went out of Serine.

'I'm not surprised, considering you lied to him about your age.'

'Why should my age make any difference?' demanded Serine petulantly. 'If I'm old enough to vote I'm old enough for anything else.'

'But not mature enough to deal with

the pressures that go with that kind of thing,' said Talia, her tone gentle now. 'Eat your breakfast and get ready. Paul's giving us a lift—unless Dervan's picking you up again.'

Serine shook her head, but she barely touched her toast, and when Paul arrived she was in the shower. Again she walked through to her bedroom with nothing but a towel wrapped seductively around her. Talia was dismayed, but Paul grinned and eyed the younger girl appraisingly.

'Good morning, Paul,' smiled Serine. 'I won't keep you waiting long.' She looked back at him over her shoulder as she went into her bedroom.

'Wow!' said Paul softly.

Talia smilingly shook her head, and although he could be a solution to her problem she nevertheless felt that she had to warn him. 'Careful, Paul. She's a man-eater.'

'She can get her teeth into me any time!' he grinned.

'She likes men with money.'

'Do you know what I think?' he said. 'That if she fell in love with the right man, then it wouldn't matter whether he had money or not.'

Talia lifted sceptical brows. 'You don't know my sister.'

'More's the pity,' he said quietly. 'But maybe I can rectify that. Do you reckon she'll let me take her out?'

'I don't know,' admitted Talia. 'But you can try.'

When Serine finally came out of her room she was wearing a white mini-skirt which revealed a long, long length of shapely leg, and a tight low-cut cotton top that was a torment for any man. Paul could not take his eyes off her. Her long auburn hair was brushed until it shone like polished copper and her wide green eyes were subtly made up and definitely provocative.

'I'm ready,' she announced gaily.

Paul gallantly gave her his arm, and

Talia followed them out of the apartment. She let Serine sit in front with Paul, and it interested her to see how Serine's mood had changed.

'Good luck with the job,' he said to Talia when they arrived at the Portakabin.

'Thank you,' she smiled.

'He's nice, isn't he?' said Serine as they walked up the steps to the office door.

'Very. Don't hurt him.'

Serine looked pained. 'As if I would!'

As soon as they were inside Dervan called Talia into his office. His tone was sharp as he invited her to sit down.

She did so with reluctance, crossing her ankles neatly, clutching her bag on her lap, wondering what was wrong now.

He stood at the window looking outside. 'Was that Paul Rogers?'

'Yes. Why?'

'You seem to be getting mighty friendly with him.' His tone was condemning, his eyes hard.

'I think that's my affair,' she said coldly.

'Did you sleep with him last night?'

Talia gasped. 'How dare you! What is this, an inquisition into my private life? I thought I'd come here to work.'

His nostrils flared. 'Did you?'

'No, I damn well did not!' she hissed.

'Whose idea was it that he pick you up this morning?'

'His, as a matter of fact.'

'Did he realise that he'd have to give Serine a lift as well?'

'Of course.'

'How old is he?'

Talia had had enough. She sprang to her feet 'I have no intention of answering any more of your questions. Please show me where I'm to work.'

Their eyes met and warred, and Talia was the first to look away.

'Is he the type you prefer?' he persisted.

'Really, Dervan, he's a friendly type, nothing more. He's a good laugh, I enjoy his company, but I don't intend to have an affair with him. Does that answer your question?'

'Will you let me take you out again?'

The sudden question surprised her, but she shook her head firmly. 'No.'

'You're still scared?' he jeered, his mouth tightening.

'I never have been.'

'Liar!'

Again she could not hold his eyes.

'I think it's you who's making a mess of your life,' he said, walking towards her and standing so close that all her pulses raced in alarm. 'Not Serine.' And with that surprising statement he led the way into his secretary's office.

Talia had no recourse but to follow and hold back the angry denial that sprang to her lips. What a nerve he'd got trying to date her when he hadn't yet finished with Serine! What sort of a man was he? The sooner she got Serine away from here the better.

The room contained two desks and a

typewriter, a drawing board and filing cabinets. Several plans of the proposed development were pinned on the walls. A small dark-haired girl looked at her with interest.

'Maria,' said Dervan, 'this is Talia, Serine's sister. She's going to help you.'

Maria looked doubtful.

'I think you'll get on well together,' he said kindly.

'I'm sure we will,' smiled Talia. 'I'm here to do whatever you ask, Maria.'

Immediately the girl relaxed. 'You are very welcome. There is so much to do I do not know which way to turn.'

Dervan patted her shoulder reassuringly. 'You're doing very well, Maria—I'm pleased with you. I'll leave you now to get acquainted. If you need another typewriter, Talia, I'll get you one.'

She nodded, and when he had gone she said bluntly to Maria, 'I know what my sister's like, you don't have to pretend to like her.'

Maria smiled hesitantly. 'She is, how can I say, very difficult to understand. I think she does not like me.'

'Not you personally, Maria. She doesn't like her own sex, she prefers men.'

'Yes, she likes Señor Deville. But I do not blame her. He is nice, do you not think so?'

'Very nice,' admitted Talia. More than nice, in fact and she wished she had met him in different circumstances.

The next few hours passed so quickly that she was amazed when Serine came to say it was lunchtime. 'Perhaps we could have a bite to eat together before you go home?'

Talia nodded, pleased that Serine was trying to make amends. She glanced towards Dervan's office as they left and Serine said 'It's no use looking for him, he's gone out. Says he won't be back today.'

Talia wondered why he hadn't told her, then decided there was no reason why he should. Probably Maria knew.

They went to the tiny pavement café Talia had used the day she had waited for Dervan. Serine ordered sandwiches and coffee, then said abruptly, 'What did Dervan want you for when he called you into his office?'

Talia shrugged. 'He was warning me about Paul again.'

'I can't imagine why,' frowned Serine. 'I thought he was rather nice myself.'

'He is,' answered Talia, adding drily, 'much nicer than Dervan, as a matter of fact.'

Serine missed the innuendo. 'You weren't talking about me again?'

Talia shook her head.

Serine smiled and relaxed and bit into her sandwich. 'I do love working here, Talia—sunshine every day. I never want to go back to England.'

'You'll have to when this job's finished.'

Serine shook her head. 'I'll move on to wherever Dervan goes next.'

'He's suggested that?' asked Talia sharply.

'Well, not exactly, but ...'

'I think you're jumping the gun,' said Talia.

'I don't. I'll soon persuade Dervan that I'm the right one for him. This is only a temporary setback.'

'Serine, no man likes to be chased. Why don't you just let go graciously?'

'It's not a crime to want something, is it?' demanded Serine.

'Of course not, for the right reasons,' answered Talia carefully. 'But you only want Dervan because he can give you all you've ever craved. Money isn't everything, Serine. When are you going to learn that?'

'I'd rather be unhappy with it than without it,' Serine insisted.

Talia shook her head. 'One day, Serine, you're going to realise that you can't always have your own way. And you're going to come down to earth with a bump.'

Serine shrugged. 'The trouble with you, Talia, is that you've no ambition.'

Talia's eyes widened. 'Ambition career-wise is one thing, Serine, ambition to marry a rich man is something else. It's a pathway to unhappiness.'

As usual Serine resented Talia's advice, and the girls finished their sandwiches in silence.

Back at the apartment Talia changed into her bikini, putting over it a short cotton skirt and a strapless sun-top, both in a beautiful sky-blue. She planned to go for a swim later, but for a while sat on the tiny terrace in front of the bungalow, her eyes closed, her mind totally occupied with Serine and Dervan.

Serine was so determined to capture him that it was doubtful Paul would get anywhere with her. Talia wondered whether to tell him not to bother trying. She even wondered whether it was worth while staying on herself. But then she thought of the way Dervan affected her.

She was as bad as her sister in that respect. And she knew she would not go.

It was obvious nothing would ever come of it, she did not even want it to; he was not the sort of man who remained faithful to one person for life. But why not indulge in a few fantasies? Surely she deserved some pleasure after all the years she had spent looking after Serine?

'One can but wonder what sort of thoughts brought that look to your face.'

Talia's eyes snapped open and a swift surge of colour warmed her cheeks. Thank goodness the human race was not far enough advanced to read thoughts. 'Dervan! What are you doing here?' He was so tall and good-looking, so heart-stoppingly male, that every nerve-end tingled with excitement.

Their eyes met and held, and Talia felt the inevitable magnetism. Then he spoke and it was gone. 'I expected to find you at the office.'

'But you said I need only work

mornings,' she protested at once, all rosy thoughts flying out of her mind.

'That's right,' he said, 'don't get on your high horse, Talia. I got back early and I was going to offer you a lift home.'

'In that case I'm glad you didn't,' she said sharply. 'I enjoyed the walk. But you still haven't told me why you're here. You didn't have to follow me to see if I came home like a good girl. What did you think, that Paul would be waiting? Were you ready to condemn him once again?'

His nostrils flared and his mouth firmed, as they always did when he was angry. 'If you choose to go out with the wrong sort then it's nothing to do with me. I've already made my feelings clear in that respect.'

'I'm glad you realise it,' Talia said tartly, 'and the sooner you realise that you're making a mistake where my sister's concerned then the better things will be all round.'

'Do you know,' he said, 'I feel sorry for

Serine if she's had to put up with this from you all her life.'

'Sorry for Serine?' she cried.

'Yes, and I would go so far as to say that you're partly responsible for the sort of person she is.'

'Me?' gasped Talia.

Dervan nodded. 'You held the reins too tightly. She was bound to rebel.'

'I did my best!' she flared.

'The trouble was,' he went on, 'you were only twelve months older than Serine is now when you had the responsibility of looking after her. You weren't really old enough to take charge. You didn't know how to handle it.'

Talia sat bolt upright in her seat. 'You have a nerve! How dare you criticise me?'

'I'm merely stating facts as I see them,' he shrugged. 'And I didn't come here to start an argument, Talia.'

'You could have fooled me,' she muttered, not intending him to hear, but he did, and he frowned.

'I came because Serine left a portfolio of important drawings here. Would you mind getting them for me?'

Talia pushed herself to her feet. 'Did she say where they are?'

'In her bedroom, by the side of the bed.'

She did not expect Dervan to follow her inside the apartment but he did, and when she came out of Serine's room with the folder in her hand he was sitting down. Nor did he make any attempt to get up when she handed it to him. 'I thought it was urgent,' she said scathingly.

'I've time for a cup of coffee, if you're going to offer me one?'

'I wasn't,' said Talia coldly, 'but if you insist.' She went through into the kitchen and filled the jug and plugged it in. She reached out cups and set them on a tray, then went back to him. 'It won't be long.'

'Good,' he smiled. 'Sit down, Talia. Tell me, are you going to spend the whole of the time you're here fighting me?'

She shrugged, sitting on the edge of a chair, her hands clenched in her lap. 'We're on opposing sides, so I suppose so.'

'It's a pity.'

She thought so too. She was more aware of him than ever. He was filling every pore, and her whole body pulsed with need of him. It was madness, it was insanity, but she had only to see him to feel like this.

'How do you feel about working for me permanently?' asked Dervan suddenly. 'Travelling with me wherever I go? I could do with a secretary who's familiar with the way I work.'

The unexpected offer made Talia look at him sharply. 'Have you asked Serine as well?'

'No,' he frowned.

'She told me that's what she's going to do.'

'I'm afraid it's all wishful thinking on her part,' he said quietly. 'Once this project's finished I shall have no further use for your sister. My next job could well be something completely different—a church, an exhibition centre, a shopping precinct; nothing that requires her talents.'

'But I'm different, am I?' Talia enquired acidly. 'Or is it that you've tired of her already? From the moment I arrived you've been making a play for me. Do you think things will be different once Serine's no longer on the scene? Is it another lover you're after? Well, for your information, I'm not interested in my sister's cast-offs. Excuse me, I think the coffee's ready.'

In the kitchen she closed the door and leaned her head against the cool paintwork. The nerve of the man! What game did he think he was playing? But how tempting his offer was. A job that would take her all over the world—it was any girl's dream. Several minutes went by before she felt sufficiently calm to take the coffee through.

'I was about to come and see what

was happening,' said Dervan, his black eyes penetrating, sending quivers down her spine as their sensual message drove home.

Talia almost dropped the tray. 'If I've kept you waiting too long then feel free to go.'

'Oh, no!' His smile was all-encompassing. 'You don't get rid of me that easily.' He stood up and took the tray from her, setting it down on the glass-topped table in front of their chairs. 'Shall I play mother? For some reason that perhaps you'd care to explain, you don't look capable.'

Talia said nothing, sitting and watching as he poured coffee into the cups. 'Milk and sugar?' he asked.

'Please.'

Instead of sliding her cup across the table he handed it to her so that she was compelled to take it from him, and when his fingers touched hers she knew it was no accident. Their eyes met as well, and Talia felt sure he knew what he was doing to her. She could deny feeling anything for him as much as she liked, but he would never believe it.

She wondered what sort of satisfaction it gave him, knowing he had the power to make any girl he liked fall in love with him. Her thoughts pulled up sharply. In love? Surely not? It was a physical attraction, that was all, the same as Serine. Love didn't enter into it.

They sipped their coffee and Dervan continued to look at her, and Talia grew more and more uncomfortable. In fact she drank her coffee so quickly that it scalded her mouth, but she wanted to get rid of him. He was filling the room with his presence, overpowering her, and the longer he stayed, the worse it would be. She could even end up not wanting him to go. The thought appalled her.

'Tell me about the sort of work you do at home.'

Talia was glad Dervan had broken the spell. 'I do all sorts of things, everything from envelopes for mailing shots to confidential reports for company executives.'

'Does it pay well?'

'Not really,' she admitted. In fact, Dervan was paying her as much as she earned in a full week.

'Then you'd be a fool to turn down my offer. I'll pay you more than double what I'm giving you now, plus living expenses.'

It was too good to be true, and Talia was truly tempted. But she shook her head. 'I can't leave Serine.'

'My God,' he snorted angrily, 'here we go again! Who's to say that Serine will come home when she's finished here? I think you'll find that she's discovered a taste for travelling and you'll hardly see her. You have no ties now, Talia. You're free at last.' He paused to let his words sink in, then said, 'Think about it.'

She would certainly do that. She could see it filling her mind for days to come. But her answer would still have to be no.

Dervan finished his coffee and stood up. Talia walked with him to the door. But, instead of taking the handle and opening it, he turned and faced her. Only inches separated them, and she could feel the heat of his body and every pulse in her raced.

'How can two sisters be so different?' he asked, reaching out and touching her hair, feather-light touches, stroking, caressing, turning Talia's insides to jelly.

She was unable to move and would have liked to put her own hand over his, bring his palm to her face, feel the warmth and strength of him, but she didn't dare. It would give too much away.

And then, using the long length of her hair, one hand each side of her head, he pulled her towards him. Talia's eyes locked into his and every inch of her body became sensitised.

His eyes were narrowed and sensual, and Talia's breath caught in her throat as his mouth drew nearer. Common sense told her to pull away, but her heart bade her otherwise.

When his lips actually touched hers his arms went around her. Here was the strength Talia had dreamed of, and she could not help herself. Her arms snaked behind his head and she returned his kiss with a wantonness that was alien to her. She drank from his mouth, she breathed him and felt him and pressed herself close.

Encouraged by her response, Dervan deepened his kiss, and her lips parted willingly, his tongue ravaging the hot moistness within. Tiny animal noises escaped the back of her throat, and she knew a wild passion she had never dreamt of.

She wanted the kiss to go on for ever and was disappointed when he lifted his mouth from hers. And maybe her disappointment showed on her face, she did not know, but Dervan said softly, 'I think you wanted that as much as me?'

'I did.' The words were out before she could stop them.

He groaned and his mouth closed on hers yet again, and many long seconds went by before he finally let her mouth go. 'If I don't stop now,' he said hoarsely, 'things could get out of hand.'

Talia agreed. He had woken in her feelings and desires that went beyond the realms of imagination. Despite the danger, she wanted more of him. Nothing had prepared her for this magical, exalting experience. But she said nothing, they simply stood and held each other, not kissing, not doing anything, simply waiting to come back down to earth.

It was a situation Talia had never found herself in before and she was not quite sure she knew how to handle it. She was certain Dervan was not interested in a committed affair, a permanent relationship; nevertheless the physical attraction was mutual.

He was in all probability, however, after

more than she was prepared to give. In fact the thought suddenly struck her, this was very likely his way of trying to persuade her to join him on his travels and live with him for a while. She had almost forgotten his earlier suggestion.

Abruptly she pulled away. 'I think it's time you went.'

Dervan frowned at her sudden movement but he at once picked up the folder and opened the door. 'What's wrong?'

'What do you mean?' she asked, purposely misunderstanding.

'The sudden tearing away from me? What ugly thought ran through your mind?' The harshness was back in his voice.

Talia looked down at her feet. 'It was blackmail, wasn't it?'

His finger on her chin brought her head up with a jerk. 'What are you talking about?'

'You're still trying to get me to join you on your travels.'

'And you think that this was—' Dervan stopped in disgust. 'I didn't realise you had quite such a low opinion of me, although I should have done. I'm sorry I ever touched you.'

Talia could have cried. 'Dervan, I didn't mean that, I—'

'Then what did you mean?' he demanded coldly.

She had no answer. She stood looking at him mutely, her eyes imploring him to understand, but after a few seconds he turned around and went out through the door.

Talia was angry with herself now for responding, for allowing him to manipulate her the same as he did all the other girls he met. She stripped off her skirt and top and, grabbing a towel, ran out to the pool, diving cleanly into the water and swimming length after length until she was completely exhausted.

She lay down on a lounger, letting the sun warm and dry her, but she felt no better. Her head began to ache, and when Serine came home from work it was throbbing.

'What took Dervan so long when he came to fetch my portfolio?' was her sister's first question.

'I gave him a cup of coffee,' answered Talia. And kissed him! And the memory of the kiss was still with her, she could almost feel his mouth on hers.

'He didn't seem in a very good mood when he came back. Had you been arguing?'

Talia shrugged. 'Don't we always? Dervan and I will never see eye to eye.'

'About me again, I suppose?' grumbled Serine sulkily.

'As a matter of fact, no,' replied Talia. 'Stop being paranoid about it!'

'Then what?'

'I'd rather not discuss it. I have a splitting headache and I'm going to lie down. If you want anything to eat you'll have to get it yourself.'

Serine stormed into her bedroom and banged the door. Seconds later she walked out stark naked and into the bathroom.

When the doorbell rang Talia feared it might be Dervan, but instead it was Paul, his cheerful grin very much in evidence.

'Come on in,' she said. 'I didn't expect you tonight.'

'I've come to see how your first day went.'

Or to see Serine? thought Talia with an inward smile. 'It wasn't bad,' she told him. 'In fact it went very well, I suppose.'

'Your boss didn't give you a hard time?'

Talia shook her head. 'He went out. I—'

Serine's voice cut into her sentence. 'Who are you talking to?'

'Paul,' she answered, with a smile at him.

The next second the door opened and Serine sauntered out with the inevitable fluffy white towel just about making her decent. Her cheeks were flushed from the shower and her hair hung in wet dripping tendrils down her back. She looked more beautiful than ever. 'Hello, Paul,' she smiled.

He could not take his eyes off her. 'Hello, Serine.'

'What are you doing here?'

'I've come to ask Talia out to dinner,' he told her. 'You can come too if you like,' adding quickly, 'If you don't mind, Talia?'

Talia liked the way he worked. It wasn't her he had come to ask out; it was Serine. 'Actually,' she said, 'I have a headache and was just about to go to bed. But you two go, by all means.'

'I thought you looked peaky.' Paul's frown of concern did not quite hide his delight. 'If you're sure you wouldn't mind?'

'Not at all,' she replied quickly.

'In that case, Serine, how about it?'

The younger girl gave a careless shrug. 'If you like.' And then to Talia, her tone hard, 'Are you sure it's not an excuse because you want to nip out to see Dervan?'

Talia glanced at her sister impatiently. 'No, it is not. I have a genuine headache.'

Not altogether convinced, Serine went through into the bedroom, glancing at Paul provocatively over her shoulder before closing the door. 'I won't be long,' she told him.

'Whew!' he said, and sat down.

Talia smiled. 'Be careful, Paul. I'd like you and Serine to be friends, but I think she might be using you. She still has her sights set on Dervan.'

'I can handle her,' he said confidently.

Talia hoped so. She liked Paul. She didn't want him hurt.

The evening went slowly after they had left. Talia took some tablets and lay down, but her headache would not go. Dervan's kisses had left her feeling like a rag doll. They had taken absolutely everything out of her. But she knew she had done the right thing in refusing to accompany him on his travels.

And when Serine came home later she was even more convinced of it. She had expected her sister to be in high spirits, she knew what good company Paul was, but Serine banged the front door and bounced into Talia's bedroom, switching on the light, regardless of the lateness of the hour and the fact that Talia could be asleep.

'What's the matter?' asked Talia, blinking as the light hurt her eyes.

'I've just seen Dervan. He was eating at the same place as Paul and me.' Serine's tone was angry, but there were tears in her eyes. 'And he was with another girl.'

CHAPTER FIVE

Serine's news shocked Talia as much as it had her sister. Dervan with another girl! Had the date been prearranged—even when he was kissing her? Talia's headache, which had abated slightly, thumped back into life. What a swine he was! Would he be asking this girl to accompany him on his travels? Didn't it matter who, so long as she was female? My God, it didn't take him long to hop from one girl to another!

'Who was it?' she asked Serine, who had sat down on the edge of her bed and was looking at her with tears streaming down her face.

'I don't know,' she sobbed. 'I've never seen her before.'

Talia put her arm around her sister's

shoulders. 'Did you speak to them?'

Serine shook her head. 'I didn't see them until I got up to go to the loo. And I don't think Dervan even saw me, he was so wrapped up in her. How could he do a thing like this to me, Talia?'

'Perhaps she's an old friend?' suggested Talia, trying to placate Serine, even though she felt just as upset about the situation. 'It could be anybody—a relative, even. You shouldn't jump to conclusions.'

'A relative?' scoffed Serine, 'when he was holding her hand across the table and looking into her eyes to the total exclusion of all else?' She blotted her eyes with a sodden handkerchief. 'She was blonde and beautiful, long hair right down her back. I hate her!'

'I think it proves,' said Talia gently, stroking Serine's hair from her face, 'that he's a man not to be trusted. I tried to tell you that in the beginning, but you wouldn't listen. He obviously tires of girls easily and slips from one to another without any compunction. You're better off without him.' *And so was she.* Dervan hadn't really been interested in her. She was a member of the opposite sex and thus fair game, and that was all there was to it.

It took Talia almost an hour to console Serine, and the next morning the younger girl announced that she felt rotten and was not going to work.

'You shouldn't let Dervan upset you like this,' said Talia gently, 'he's not worth it.'

'It's not him,' replied Serine. 'I simply feel lousy.'

Talia knew she was lying, but she didn't press the matter. 'Can I get you anything?' she asked instead.

'A cup of black coffee and some toast. Please.'

When Paul arrived to pick them up he was instantly concerned to hear Serine was in bed. 'What's wrong with her?' he wanted to know. 'She was all right last night. Was it something she ate?'

'Dervanitis,' said Talia sharply.

He frowned, then laughed ruefully. 'I see. But is it going to help, staying away? Surely she'll risk losing her job?'

'Personally I don't think that would be a bad thing,' said Talia. 'She was pretty upset when she came in last night.'

'She was more than that at the restaurant,' he said. 'I had to physically restrain her from going and bashing him with her handbag!' He smiled at the thought. 'She has spirit, your sister. She's quite a girl.'

'Serine's afraid she's lost everything that she's been angling after,' said Talia, 'and she'll do her damnedest to get Dervan back—you mark my words. She won't give in that easily. She's upset now, but she'll come fighting back. You're not in with a chance, Paul, unless you've got a few million stashed away?'

He grinned. 'You never know, I might win the football pools. Do you think I ought to stay and look after Serine?'

'I think,' said Talia, 'that as soon as we've gone she'll be out of bed like a shot. She's not really ill, it's just her feelings that are hurt.' And so were hers, though she knew better than to show it.

'Then maybe I'll be able to persuade her to go out with me later.' He looked pleased at the thought.

Talia said goodbye to Serine and they left and it amused her to see how anxious Paul was to get back. She hoped Serine wouldn't hurt him; he was too nice.

She went straight to Dervan's office, and as his door was open she tapped lightly and walked inside. He looked up from his desk, and Talia could not prevent her heart from skipping a beat. She could smell his aftershave, and feel the inevitable magnetism, and knew that if she had not been so mistrusting she could have been the girl out with him last night.

He smiled, seeming pleased to see her, and his smile jangled her nerve-ends, but

Talia guessed his mood had nothing at all to do with her. They had parted yesterday on a sour note, and it was unlikely that he had forgiven her.

'Serine's not coming in today,' she said at once.

His black brows rose. 'Is she ill?'

'She's upset,' answered Talia. 'She went out with Paul last night and guess who she saw dining in the same restaurant?'

His eyebrows lifted. 'I thought Paul was your—er—boyfriend?'

'Friend,' she corrected coldly.

'Some friend, if he takes off with your sister!'

'It was at my suggestion. He came to invite me out but I had a headache.'

'Paul should be careful,' remarked Dervan. 'That cat's got claws, and once she digs them in she's reluctant to let go.'

'Serine's had one date with him, for heaven's sake, what are you talking about?'

'One date leads to another, and Paul

doesn't look as though he has the means to keep your sister in the manner she expects. Perhaps I'll go and visit Serine—I wanted her to finish some specifications today. If she intends to be childish and carry on like this I shall have to think about finding a replacement.'

'I don't think she'll be very happy to see you. You're not on her list of favourite people right at this moment.' And personally Talia thought his going to see her a stupid idea.

'I couldn't care less about that!' he snarled, standing up and glaring at her. 'I pay Serine to do a job and I expect her to do it. Personal gripes shouldn't enter into it.'

'You can't blame her for being offended,' she said. 'After all, you were pretty thick before I came on the scene.'

'We were never *pretty thick*, as you put it. I took her out a few times, yes, and maybe flirted with her—she's a pretty girl—but I also made it clear that I wasn't serious. I assumed she understood that but apparently not.'

'The last thing she wants at this moment is you breathing down her throat,' said Talia.

'Are you sticking up for her?' Dervan asked incredulously. 'I thought you wanted us to break up?'

'You could have done it more gently,' she reproved. 'You're forgetting how young and inexperienced she is.'

'I wouldn't let Serine hear you say that,' he said wryly. 'She thinks she's quite the grown-up lady.' He smiled. 'She ought to take a leaf out of her sister's book. I can't imagine you taking a day off work because you'd seen the man you thought you were in love with out with someone else. You'd rise above it.'

He stood very close to her, and Talia's heart began to beat erratically. 'I'm sure I would,' she said, hoping he did not notice the strange wobble in her voice.

His hands came down on her shoulders.

'As I said yesterday, Talia, it's hard to believe that you're sisters. Have you thought any more about my offer?'

She wished he hadn't touched her and she had to force into her mind the picture of him with a long-haired blonde. 'It really doesn't require much thought,' she said distantly.

He frowned. 'I shan't give up.'

Then what were you doing with that girl last night? Talia wanted to ask. Unless he really did mean that he wanted her as his secretary and nothing more? Perhaps she had put the wrong interpretation on it? But if so, why had he kissed her? Confusion filled Talia's mind and she tried to pull away from him, but his grip tightened and his head came down.

Talia could not believe his audacity and her eyes shot sparks, but she maintained her dignity and let him kiss her. It was a nothing affair compared with yesterday afternoon, but nevertheless it recreated all the same sensations, and when Dervan calmly walked out of the office a few seconds later her legs threatened to buckle beneath her.

And it was not until then she realised he had said nothing about the girl he was with. Not even an excuse. He had ignored the whole issue.

'What is wrong?' asked Maria a few minutes later when Talia walked through into her office.

'I'm worried about Serine,' she lied. 'She's not well.'

'She will be all right. Spanish tummy, I expect. It affects most English people.'

As Talia sorted and filed letters she listened for Dervan to return. He was a long time. She wondered if Paul had been with Serine when he got there. It could be an interesting situation. She even allowed herself a little smile.

When she finally heard him mounting the cabin steps she stopped what she was doing and waited, thinking he might come and speak to her. But his door slammed shut and there was silence. Talia felt trepidation. What had Serine said?

She did not see him again before finishing work for the day, and when she got back to the apartment she was not surprised to find it empty. Perhaps this was what Dervan had found? If that was the case then it served Serine right and she deserved to lose her job.

It was late evening before Serine and Paul returned. She was laughing and looked happy enough, and Paul too seemed as though he had had a good time. 'I can see I have no need to ask if you're feeling better,' Talia remarked.

Serine shrugged. 'There's no point in moping. But I haven't given up. How's Dervan?'

'You should know, he came to see you, didn't he?' asked Talia shortly. 'Or weren't you in? Was that the reason he was in a foul mood when he got back?'

'This sounds like a personal conversation,' cut in Paul. 'I think I'll go. I'll see you in the morning.'

'Thanks for today,' said Serine. 'It was just what I needed.' She kissed him full on the lips and he hugged her, looked awkwardly at Talia, and then left. It meant nothing to Serine and everything to Paul. Talia felt sorry for him.

Serine lay down on the settee, her hands behind her head, looking up at the ceiling. 'I did see Dervan, yes. Actually I was quite surprised—I never expected him. But it's not over between us.'

Talia looked sharply at her sister. 'Don't say he's asked you out again?'

'Not yet but he will,' Serine replied confidently. 'I've got rid of the opposition.'

'What do you mean?' asked Talia sharply.

'Well, first of all I just happened to bump into that girl he was with last night.'

Talia frowned.

'Yes, she's a courier. She turned up here this morning with a coachload of holidaymakers.' Serine looked at her sister sheepishly. 'I sort of let it drop that Dervan belonged to me. She was most apologetic. I don't think he'll be seeing her again.'

'Oh, Serine, was that wise? If she should tell him then it's you who'll be in trouble.'

'I don't think she will,' said Serine confidently. 'Don't worry, we parted on good terms. Actually she's a nice girl. I feel sorry for her.' She paused a moment. 'And then there's you.'

Talia's eyes shot wide. 'Me?'

'Well, I thought it only right that Dervan should know how often you've been out with Paul and how much he's beginning to mean to you. I think I can safely say that Dervan won't show any more interest in you.'

'Oh, Serine, how could you? You know it's not true.'

'All's fair in love and war, as they say,' shrugged Serine airily. 'I didn't think you'd mind anyway, I know you don't care for him.'

Talia opened her mouth to deny it, then closed it again. What was the point?

'I think I'll go to bed now,' said Serine sweetly. 'I've had quite an exhausting day one way and another. It's a pity Paul has no money—he's quite a guy. I could fall for him.'

'He's certainly more your type than Dervan,' said Talia wearily, but it didn't matter what she said, Serine would go her own way.

What hurt her most was that there was absolutely no hope for her now where Dervan was concerned. She really might as well pack up and go home.

She went to work as usual the next day, ready to do battle, ready to defend herself against anything Dervan might say. But he ignored her. And it wouldn't have hurt so much if he hadn't spent a considerable amount of time in Serine's office. The thought of the two of them together curled Talia's stomach in knots.

That night she accepted Paul's invitation

to join him for dinner. Serine said she was going out, and Talia didn't ask her where.

Instead of their usual haunts in Puerto del Carmen they found a nightclub in Arrecife. It was a smart-looking place and Talia wondered whether Paul could afford it, but when she suggested going dutch he was offended.

'I'm sorry things aren't working out between you and Serine,' she said.

He grinned. 'I'm living in hope.'

Talia shook her head. 'I don't understand you, Paul. Doesn't it put you off, seeing her jealous streak?'

'I wish it were me she was after so determinedly.'

'She does like you—she told me so.'

'She does?' His eyes lit up. 'Then there's hope for me yet!'

The evening passed slowly. They dined and danced. They watched a floor show and wandered into the casino. They didn't spend anything. Neither had money to lose, but it was fascinating watching.

Then Talia became aware of someone watching her. She looked across the room and met Dervan's eyes. Even with all the people surrounding them there was still that magnetic pull, and it was a few seconds before she looked away.

She tried to ignore him, tried to fix all her attention on Paul and the game of roulette they were watching, but it was not long before she felt compelled to look in his direction once again.

This time he was not watching her. He was looking at his companion instead. Talia had not noticed her before. She was a blonde in a white lurex dress that plunged almost to her navel. The same girl? The courier? But it couldn't be, because this one had short hair, and Serine had said the other girl's was waist-length.

Paul felt her go tense and he followed the direction of her eyes. 'Damn!' he swore uncharacteristically. 'I didn't expect this. Who the hell's the guy with now? I must say he believes in sharing himself around a bit. Do you want to go?'

'No, but I'd like to dance,' answered Talia. She needed to get out of the room.

But on the dance floor there was no escape either. When a hand touched her shoulder she knew immediately who it was. 'Excuse me,' Dervan said to Paul, and swept Talia away before either of them could do anything about it.

She clamped her lips and said nothing, matching her steps to his, finding it surprisingly easy to follow him. It was as though they had always danced together.

His hand in the small of her back propelled her close to him, and she inhaled his now familiar musky smell. Whatever happened in the future, she would always think of Dervan whenever she smelled this particular brand of aftershave.

'I didn't realise,' he said, 'that you and Paul frequented places like this.'

His head was bent to her, but Talia

steadfastly refused to meet his eyes, staring over his shoulder instead. She could see Paul across the other side of the room talking to Dervan's blonde friend. He looked ill at ease and his eyes kept following her around the room. She smiled at him and guessed he was wondering how soon he could rescue her. Or maybe he thought she did not want to be rescued? Maybe he thought she was enjoying dancing with Dervan?

'It's the first time,' she answered. 'And to be frank, I wouldn't have come if I'd known you were going to be here.'

'Why?' he asked, letting go her hand and lifting her chin so that she was compelled to look at him. 'Do I still—disturb you?' The pause was deliberate.

'In more ways than one.' she snapped, and tried to turn her head away, but his grip was invincible. He was going to make sure that she did not avoid his eyes. Did he know the power they held? Was he aware that she sometimes felt she was drowning in their depths? He looked only at her. She was the only person in the room so far as he was concerned, and he expected her to give him the same attention.

'Why are you doing this?' she asked. 'What's your friend going to think? It's certainly not very gentlemanly to dance with someone else.'

'I explained the situation.' His lips quirked with amusement. 'Zoe understands perfectly.'

'What situation?' demanded Talia with a frown.

Dervan ignored her question, saying instead, 'Tell me, Talia, why did you lie to me about Paul? Why didn't you tell me exactly how much he meant to you?'

About to declare yet again that Paul meant nothing to her and that Serine had been lying, Talia had second thoughts. If he was of the opinion that she and Paul had something going then he might leave her alone. It would be the best solution all round. It was hard to stomach that she was one of many girls in his life, but if that was the case then she wanted nothing more to do with him.

'I didn't actually lie,' she said at length. 'He didn't mean anything to me in the beginning.'

'But now?' His black eyes were intent on hers.

'Now I feel differently about him.'

'How different?'

Talia hesitated. Why was he being so persistent? Why couldn't he leave her alone? 'We get on very well together.'

'So well that you let him take your sister out?' he asked tersely.

'I trust him.' Her eyes widened in defiance.

'Maybe, but can Serine be trusted? There was certainly nothing platonic in their relationship the other night. They were, to put it crudely, all over each other.'

'So you did see them?' accused Talia.

He nodded. 'But of course.'

'Serine thought you hadn't.'

'I didn't want to spoil her obvious enjoyment.'

'Spoil her enjoyment?' echoed Serine incredulously. 'When you take another girl out before you've even had the common decency to tell Serine it's all over.'

'There was never anything started, so I don't see how I can end it,' said Dervan. 'Are you sticking up for her again?'

'No, I am not!' she cried. 'But you must admit it was a pretty calculated thing to do. And now tonight you've got another girl in tow. How many more will there be?'

'As many as it takes,' he answered calmly.

Talia didn't bother to ask what he meant. It was clear. As many as it took to satisfy him.

'Will you tell Serine?' he asked.

'Of course,' she snapped. 'I want her to know exactly what a swine you are!'

His hand was making slow, caressing

circles over the naked skin of her back and he was inching her even closer towards him. Talia could hardly credit what he was doing. What a rat he was! It was evidently his technique to make every girl feel special during the time he was with her. Well, not this girl. Not any more. She had learned enough about him in the last few days to put her off him forever.

She tried to pull away, but something in her expression must have warned him, for his arms tightened almost before she made her move. 'What's wrong?' His eyes glittered into hers. 'Still fighting the urge to give in to me?'

'I have no need!' she spat. 'The urge has already gone.'

'Why don't I believe you?'

She shrugged. 'Please yourself what you believe. It happens to be true.'

'Perhaps I should put it to the test?'

Her eyes widened in alarm.

'But not here,' Dervan said. 'I'll save you the embarrassment of struggling in public. Not that I think you'd fight me for long.'

'Don't be too sure,' she hissed.

His lips quirked. 'Maybe I ought to kiss you now?'

'You dare!' Talia struggled to free herself, but to no avail.

'You're very beautiful when you're angry, did you know that? Much more beautiful than your sister.'

'Flattery won't get you anywhere,' she snapped.

'I'm speaking the truth, Talia. Serine's beauty is only skin-deep. Yours comes from inside. Your face lights up from within when you smile—you're radiant.'

'Why are you telling me these things?' she asked crossly. 'Do you think it's going to make a difference to how I feel about you?'

'I'm telling you because I think you ought to know. From what you've told me, there haven't been many men in your life, and I doubt whether there've been any who've treated you as you deserve.'

And he was an expert on women. Was that what he was telling her? Nevertheless he made her feel good, and she was almost sorry when the dance came to an end. But when he led her back to Paul and asked him whether they would like to join them at their table, swift dismay took the place of pleasure.

She gave Paul an anxious glance—but too late; he was already agreeing.

'Why did you do that?' she hissed through her teeth as they made their way to the far corner of the room.

'I thought you looked as though you were enjoying yourself. Was I wrong?'

'Totally,' she snapped, and clutching his arm, 'Let's go.'

Paul pulled a rueful face. 'I don't think we can now. But we needn't stay long.'

'You bet we won't!'

Although Talia sat next to Paul she was opposite Dervan, and he took no pains to hide his interest in her. Talia thought it odd that he should act like this in front of Zoe, but the girl showed no sign of jealousy. In fact she was perfectly willing to talk to Paul.

Dervan ordered drinks, and after a few moments' general conversation he asked Paul what he did for a living.

'I'm a computer analyst,' he answered easily.

'That's interesting. I was actually thinking of installing a computer here to link up with the one in my London office. Perhaps you could advise me?'

Paul looked surprised that Dervan should seek his advice, and Talia was suspicious, feeling sure there was some ulterior motive behind Dervan's request. She hoped Paul would refuse, but no—he nodded happily. 'Any time.'

Dervan looked pleased. 'Come and see me on Monday morning.' And to Talia, 'Can you operate a computer?'

'I had training at college,' she admitted, 'also in word processing, but I'm no expert. I haven't used one in a long time.' Why he was asking her Talia did not know, she would be gone from here long before his system was installed.

Her question was answered. 'Would you contemplate staying on a little longer? Maria knows nothing about computers. She could do with your help.'

'I don't think so,' she said quietly. What was it with this man? Why was be being so insistent that she work for him?

'I'll make it worth your while.'

Talia did not doubt that he would, but she knew it would be insanity to agree.

'Give it some thought,' he said, when she did not answer.

By this time Zoe was back in conversation with Paul. Dervan never took his eyes off Talia, and once again she found it difficult to look away. His magnetism was stronger than ever.

When she reached out for her glass his hand came across the table and touched hers. She looked quickly at the others, but they did not notice. Unwanted tremors ran through her and her toes curled inside her sandals. Would she ever be able to face Dervan without feeling excited by him? And the trouble was, he knew what he was doing to her. He was proving what she had tried to deny. 'Let's dance again,' he said quietly.

Talia could not say no. She rose as if in a dream and slipped into his arms, making no attempt now to pull away when he held her close. Every inch of their bodies, from thigh to chest touched. Talia closed her eyes and wallowed in the sheer sensationalism Dervan was creating, and when he lifted her chin she parted her lips to meet his without stopping to think about the rightness of it all. It was no good denying it: he had the power to make her do whatever he wanted. She was putty in his hands.

Without knowing how it happened, Talia found herself outside in the splendid gardens at the back of the nightclub. A silver moon hung in the sky, acting host to the myriad stars who danced court to her. Palm trees waved their fronds in the breeze and ornamental grasses shivered.

Still holding her close, Dervan brought their bodies to a standstill. His hands cupped her face and he looked deep into her eyes. He gently touched her brows, following their outline, her straight nose, the contours of her cheeks, every inch of her face, her mouth, pulling down her lower lip and kissing the silky-smooth flesh inside.

Talia wriggled against him, unconsciously gyrating her hips, unable to contain the excitement he was arousing inside her.

His hand dropped lower, caressing the line of her throat, finding the pulse that behaved erratically at its base. His voice was gruff when he spoke. 'Tell me now, Talia, that Paul means more to you than I do.'

It still puzzled her why he was so

determined to start something between them. He had once said she intrigued him. Was that it? Didn't she respond as easily as most other girls? Was his pride wounded? 'Is this a test?' she asked, though she could not put the anger into her voice that she would have liked. She was enjoying herself too much.

'No test, Talia,' he answered. 'Just a quest for the truth.'

'The truth,' she told him bluntly, 'is that I find you a very, very sexy man. But you know that, don't you? However, you can rest assured that my emotions aren't involved.'

'As they are with Paul?' he growled.

How could she say yes when his mouth was following the line of his hands, his tongue trailing down her throat, touching the pulse, moving even lower to the hollow between her breasts?

It had been a mistake putting on a low-cut dress, an even bigger one allowing him to persuade her to buy it. 'Dervan!' Her fingers bit into his shoulders. *'Dervan!'* It was a groan of ecstasy, not a request for him to stop.

'Dervan, what?' he asked, looking into her face, his eyes glazed with desire.

'Why are you doing this to me?'

'Don't you like it?' He nibbled her ear.

'Yes.' *Madly!* 'Yes, of course I do.' It would be pointless lying when he could feel her complete arousal. 'But what are you after? You can have Serine any time you want and probably Zoe and that other girl. Why me?'

'Because, my dear sweet Talia, you are the one I want, not the others.'

She eyed him disbelievingly. 'I don't understand. If it were just me you wanted you wouldn't bother with anyone else. I don't want to be one of a crowd. I think we should go back inside.' And what exactly did he mean by *wanted?* He wanted to have an affair? He wanted to take her to bed? Was that it? Was that what all this was leading up to? She really must learn not to let him get through to her like this.

'Trust me, Talia.' His eyes held hers. 'I don't want to hurt you. I want us to be together.'

'I don't,' she cried, 'not in the way you're suggesting!' Using all her strength, she broke free and ran back towards the building.

'Talia, wait!'

But she ignored him and did not stop until she was inside. Paul and Zoe were dancing, but the moment Paul spotted Talia he came across to her. 'Take me home,' she pleaded.

He frowned at the high colour in her cheeks and the over-brightness of her eyes. 'What's wrong?' he asked.

'Nothing, I just want to go.'

Dervan approached them and Paul looked at him questioningly, but the older man gave nothing away. In fact there was nothing at all in his expression to suggest that he had been deeply aroused only a few moments earlier.

Talia wouldn't look at him, she kept tugging at Paul's arm, and Zoe was glancing from one to the other in total confusion.

But as soon as they were outside and in Paul's hired car he insisted on knowing what was wrong.

'Dervan made a pass at me,' she said bluntly.

His brows slid up. 'And you objected? I'm surprised. I thought you and he were getting on like a house on fire. It looked that way. Was I wrong?'

'No, not really,' admitted Talia reluctantly. 'But then I began to think about Zoe and Serine and that other girl, and I thought why should I be another statistic?'

'So you slapped him across the face and told him to stop it?'

She smiled. 'Not exactly, but it might have been a good idea.'

He put his hand over hers. 'Poor Talia! In love with a man who's only interested in a sexual relationship.'

'I am not!' she cried indignantly. 'In love with Dervan? Me? Nonsense!'

'No?' he asked quietly.

'Well, maybe a little bit,' she admitted, after a great deal of soul-searching.

She closed her eyes and rested her head on the back of the seat. What a fool to fall in love with a man like Dervan. What a mindless idiot. There could be nothing permanent in it. There was no permanence in his life whatsoever. That was the way he wanted and liked it. And although he might be attracted to her he had no intention of ever falling in love. That was not a part of his plan at all.

CHAPTER SIX

At Talia's insistence Paul took Serine out on Saturday while she stayed and lazed beside the pool. It was heaven having absolutely nothing to do. The only cloud in an otherwise blue sky was Dervan.

She was all mixed up where he was concerned, she did not know what she wanted. No, that was wrong, she did know. She was in love with him, much as she fought against the idea, and she wanted a committed relationship. But that was impossible. Dervan wanted her for as long as it took him to get fed up, and Talia did not think she could accept that kind of an affair.

On Sunday Paul and Serine went out again—this time it was their own choice. Paul made sure first of all that Talia did not mind, but there was no way she could object if it meant Serine was being kept happy. The last thing she wanted was her sister bemoaning her fate regarding Dervan. Serine had not accepted kindly the news that he had been out with yet another girl.

Talia was feeling deliciously hot and lazy when a shadow fell across her body. At first she thought the sun had gone behind a cloud, but when she opened her eyes it was Dervan who stood there. Fully dressed, he looked out of place among the semi-nude sun-worshippers. A faint frown creased his brow. 'Where's your sister?' he asked.

'Out with Paul,' answered Talia, glad he could not see the sudden frenetic beating of her heart. How good he looked in mint-green linen trousers and a green and white striped shirt! She had been lying down thinking about him, and now he was here. Devastating her.

'Don't you mind?' The frown deepened.

'Why should I?' She pushed herself up

on her elbows and tried to pretend an indifference she was far from feeling.

'What's happened to the budding romance?' he mocked. 'Don't tell me it's over already? What went wrong? Was Paul unable to resist Serine's undoubted charms? Has he transferred his affections?'

'Of course not,' she snapped. 'But she's feeling pretty bad about you, and—'

'Paul's doing his best to console her?' he cut in drily. 'What a marvellous excuse! And neither of them cares that you're out on a limb?'

'I'm not complaining,' she said. Especially now. Even if Dervan turned round and disappeared it would not matter. She had seen him and that was enough, enough to set her adrenalin racing and her thoughts rioting.

'Get up,' he said abruptly. 'We're going out.'

Talia frowned, but really she was pleased by his suggestion. Inside she was bubbling with secret pleasure. This was her last weekend before going home. Five more mornings in his office and then that was it. Back to England. Why not enjoy what he was offering?' It could do no harm, so long as she remembered that it meant nothing to him and that tomorrow he would probably be taking out someone else. But at least she would have memories to treasure.

He held out his hand and Talia took it, trying her hardest to ignore the tingles of sensitivity that ran through her at his touch. 'I'll have to go and put something on,' she said when she was standing.

Dervan took a long, slow look at her, from the tips of her toes right up to her eyes, missing nothing in between. The bronze bikini was brief, and Talia felt an ache of need spread in her groin. Hell, what was she doing? She ought to refuse. It could be disastrous. She would never be able to hide her feelings for the whole day.

'It's a pity,' he said, 'but I suppose you

must. Bring your bikini, though, in case we go swimming.'

Talia almost ran back to her apartment and it took her but a few seconds to pull on a wrap-around dress. She left her bikini underneath; if they should go swimming she did not want to undress in front of him. She popped a few things into her bag and pronounced herself ready.

'That must constitute a record,' said Dervan, appraising her slowly. 'I've never known a woman get ready so quickly!'

Talia grew warm. She hoped he didn't think her too eager. She ought to have taken her time, kept him waiting a few minutes. 'Why waste the day?' she said lightly.

'Why indeed?' His hand cupped her elbow as they walked to his car and yet again her stomach fluttered and her skin prickled. Thinking about him had been enough to send her body into physical chaos, but now that he was here, and actually touching her, and they were about to spend the whole day together, it turned into a positive quagmire of emotion.

They drove through Macher to Uga, where Talia saw camels grazing on the hillside. At first she could not believe her eyes. 'Camels?' she enquired incredulously.

Dervan laughed. 'They're stabled here. There are over a hundred at Timanfaya giving rides to tourists.'

The next place was Yaiza, reputedly the most beautiful village on the island. It was spotlessly clean, with snowy-white buildings and brilliant flowers whichever way you looked. There were geranium plants as big as shrubs, covered in a mass of blood-red blooms. Palms that were not much taller than Talia, the trunks looking like overgrown pineapples. Cacti with orange flowers resembling red-hot pokers. It was very impressive.

They turned off here on to a long, straight road, eventually passing a sign announcing that this was Timanfaya National Park. The Fire Mountains. Talia glanced about her with total fascination. In the distance were the mountains, here, on either side, was mile upon mile of black petrified lava. It was an awesome sight.

Dervan stopped the car and she got out. He stood beside her. It was total devastation—not a blade of grass, not a green leaf to be seen anywhere. Nothing but a sea of black volcanic rock. And silence. No birds, no wildlife, just the metalled road that had been carved straight through it. Talia wished she had brought her camera. But who had thought when she left England, however long ago it was—it seemed like a lifetime—that she would be spending her time sightseeing?

'Can you imagine,' he said, his voice close to her ear, sending fresh shivers of sensation through her veins, 'when the whole of this was a sea of running molten lava?'

Talia nodded. 'It's frightening. It's incredible! I keep thinking of the villages that lie buried. I've never seen anything like it.'

'No one can argue with the force of nature.'

Nor could she argue with the force of his magnetism. It never lessened—in the car, out of it an inch away, a mile away. Always she felt it. She turned to him and he was looking at her, and she did not have time to hide the blatant desire she felt so strongly.

His eyes darkened and he put a firm finger beneath her chin, lifting her face up to his, kissing her full on the lips. Talia's whole being was set on fire, but the kiss was disappointingly brief. 'I think now is neither the time nor the place,' he said. 'Later, maybe. We'll find ourselves a nice secluded little spot and ...' He did not finish his sentence, leaving Talia to draw her own conclusion.

They got back into his car, Talia's body throbbing with a raw desire she found alien and yet welcome, and although she still looked out at the passing scenery she now saw little of it. Dervan occupied her mind to the exclusion of all else.

A few kilometres further on they came across the camel caravans, each line of over a dozen camels sitting patiently waiting for the next group of tourists. Each animal had a green-painted wooden seat slung and strapped on either side of its hump. 'Would you like a ride?' asked Dervan, but Talia declined. It looked far from comfortable, and she would much rather be sitting next to him in his car than with the camel's hump between them.

Eventually they reached the place where all tourists gather, where the temperature in the mountains at ground level was reputed to be around four hundred and twenty-five degrees Celsius. In the restaurant food was cooking on grids over holes in the ground, and Talia could feel the heat as she stood and watched chicken portions steadily browning. 'Free heat,' she said to Dervan. 'We could all do with that.'

And outside attendants were entertaining the crowd by throwing into fissures in the volcanic rock small branches which instantly set on fire. Cinders scooped from a few inches below ground were too hot to handle, and water, poured down a tube into the earth, spouted out as steam a few seconds later. 'It's incredible,' she said. 'I'm so glad you brought me.' The fact that she had run away from him on Friday night was already forgotten.

'And I'm glad you came,' he smiled, putting his arm about her shoulders. 'But if you've seen enough we'll move on. I prefer you to myself.'

Fresh frissons of awareness ran through her, and she felt as though she was walking on cloud nine as they headed back to the car. What a wonderful day this was turning out to be! Already she had forgotten that it meant nothing to him.

Dervan drove to the coast this time, to a long stretch of sand with hardly another person in sight, and surprisingly he produced a picnic hamper.

Talia's eyes widened and a sudden painful suspicion crept into her happiness. 'Who did you plan to entertain when you packed that?' The words were out before she could stop them. After all, it was Serine he had asked for when he turned up that morning.

'Really, Talia,' he mocked. 'Do you need to ask?'

'Yes, I do,' she said, more sharply perhaps than she intended. 'No girl likes to feel she's second choice.'

He frowned, his brows drawing together into a thick jagged line. When he spoke again his voice had a hard edge to it. 'I can assure you, Talia, that it was my intention all along to ask you.'

'Not Serine?'

He shook his head, his mouth grim.

'Not the girl you were with the other night?'

'Most definitely not.'

Talia looked down at her feet, suddenly

feeling a complete and utter fool. 'I'm sorry,' she muttered.

'Being sorry makes no difference to the fact that you were ready to condemn me,' he rasped.

'You must admit I have every reason,' she protested. 'You appear to take out a different girl every day.'

'Today I wanted to take you out. No one else, just you. Maybe you haven't realised it yet, but I happen to prefer your company.'

'I don't believe that,' said Talia quickly. 'I'm a fresh face, someone to entertain you temporarily, but that's all.'

His nostrils flared. 'Is that what you really think?'

Talia shrugged. 'What else is there to think?'

Dervan shook his head in anger. 'Let's forget the whole thing and eat. Either that or go home.'

Because she had hit on the truth! Talia staged a quick mental battle. She wanted to stay, she really did, but would it be wise? Had the rot set in? Would they continue to bicker at each other for the rest of the day? Oh, why hadn't she kept her mouth shut? She had been enjoying herself so much.

'Well, Talia?' he asked impatiently.

His face was implacable and she could see that the picnic was doomed, but somehow she heard herself saying, 'I'd like to stay.' She deeply regretted being so outspoken but knew that an apology, no matter how sincere, would not be accepted. She had shown her distrust of him all too clearly.

'Very well.' He spread a blanket on the sand and opened the hamper. It was full of good things to eat, but Talia only nibbled, tasting nothing, sadly looking out to sea, lost in a world of her own misery.

Dervan on the other hand showed a ravenous hunger, and by the time he had finished there was very little left in the basket. He had packed wine and they drank it between them, and afterwards Talia lay back on the sand and closed her eyes.

'It's bad for your digestion.'

She looked up at him. 'What is?'

'Lying down after a meal. I suggest we go for a walk.'

It was the first time he had spoken, and the hardness had gone out of his voice. It wasn't quite normal, nevertheless it was an attempt at making the peace.

Talia smiled and sat up. 'I'd love to.'

He stowed everything in the boot of his car and as they walked along the shore he began to talk about his development. 'It's by far my most ambitious project yet. I spent ages searching for the right location. It had to face south, and I wanted it to slope right down to the seashore so that every single property gets the maximum amount of sunshine.'

Talia had seen the plans on his office wall and knew exactly what he was talking about. 'It will be perfect.'

'I hope so. I have a lot of money invested in it. It's been my lifelong ambition to design and build something like this. I'm aiming to blend local architectural traditions with twentieth-century living standards. No two apartments will be alike—entrances in different positions, variously shaped terraces, a choice of furnishing, etcetera.'

'It's exciting,' smiled Talia. 'I wish I had Serine's talent. It would be lovely to be completely involved in something like this.' She spoke almost without thinking, not realising how Dervan would interpret her words.

'You still have the chance of joining my team. I'm serious about installing a computer.'

But that was all it would be, a working relationship. She had blown her chances of anything else. Not that there had ever been any real hope for her. Dervan had proved that he was not a one-woman man, and no matter how many times he professed to prefer her company she would never believe him.

The trouble was, her heart did not always know what her mind was thinking. Even at this moment she was responding to his nearness. It was insanity—and to even contemplate staying on and working for him was courting disaster.

'I don't think so,' she said, 'but I'll give it some thought.' She skipped to one side as the crystal-clear water lapped further up the shore.

'Personally,' he said, joining her, 'I can't see what there is to think about. What would you be giving up? A job that pays peanuts.'

'And my house.'

'Rent it out. Or sell and buy another when you're ready for it.'

'You make it sound so simple,' Talia sighed.

'It is. It's you who keeps putting obstacles in the way. What is it that you've got against me, apart from thinking I'm a womaniser?'

Talia shrugged. 'Nothing.'

He stopped walking. 'That's something at least.'

Their eyes met and held for a few seconds, then Dervan suggested they turn back and go for a swim.

The rest of the day passed relatively smoothly. He was friendly, charming, polite, courteous, but not lover-like. He did not attempt to kiss her again, and Talia wished with all her heart that she had not been so frank. Earlier in the day she had had the feeling that something was ready to develop between them. Nonsense probably, but even so they had established a happy rapport. Now it was a wary relationship, Talia trying hard not to upset him again, Dervan being carefully polite.

When they got back to her apartment she did not ask him in, afraid he might refuse, which would hurt her even more. 'Thank you for today,' she said. 'I'm sorry if I upset you. It wasn't intentional.'

'Don't let it worry you,' he said. 'Goodbye. I'll see you at the office tomorrow.'

Serine appeared in the doorway as Talia walked up the short path, and judging by the expression on her face she was not in a very good mood. Talia was surprised to see her. Yesterday it had been almost midnight when Paul brought her back. What time was it now—about five? She glanced at her watch. A quarter past. Something must have happened.

The second Talia stepped inside she discovered what it was. 'How dare you go out with Dervan?' accused Serine shrilly.

Talia gave an inward groan. Another confrontation with her sister over Dervan was the last thing she wanted. 'I'm sorry, but—'

'Sorry?' demanded Serine. 'Is this why you suggested I go out with Paul—because you had it planned? Did you go out with him yesterday as well?'

'No, Serine, of course I didn't,' answered Talia patiently. 'And none of it was arranged. I was totally surprised when he turned up here this morning.'

Serine clearly did not believe her. 'Why did he ask you out? He knows about you and Paul.'

'But Paul wasn't here, was he?'

'What's happened to the girl he was with on Friday night?'

'I've no idea,' answered Talia.

Serine's eyes were accusing. 'I think you and Dervan are holding out on me. I think that those other girls were arranged to throw the scent off you.'

Talia felt like laughing, it was so ridiculous. 'Heavens, Serine, what nonsense! I don't know the first thing about them, and there's absolutely nothing between Dervan and me. And nothing between you and him either, so why don't you stop behaving as though you own him?'

'There would be, if it weren't for you,'

wailed Serine, some of the aggression going out of her. 'If you hadn't turned up he'd have probably asked me to marry him by now.'

'I don't think so,' Talia replied, 'and if you'll excuse me, Serine, I'd like to go and take a shower.' Much as she loved her sister, she found it difficult to be patient with her in these moods.

Paul turned up again later and took Serine out. Talia spent a quiet evening on her own going over her day with Dervan, on the one hand regretting what she had said to him, on the other knowing that it had been the truth anyway, and it was best he knew it.

As arranged, Paul accompanied the girls into the office the next morning and spent a considerable length of time with Dervan. Talia began to think they would never come out. When they did it was almost lunchtime, and Serine, who must also have been waiting for them to emerge, came out of her own room and caught hold of

Paul's arm, gazing adoringly up into his face. 'You're just in time to take me to lunch,' she told him.

Through the open doorway Talia saw Dervan frown at Serine's enthusiasm.

'You will take me, Paul, won't you?' she went on. 'You have finished talking about computers?'

'As a matter of fact,' said Dervan drily, 'Paul is lunching with me.'

'I'm terribly sorry, darling,' Paul confessed, 'but I promise we'll go somewhere extra nice tonight to make up.'

Serine pouted, but when he kissed her she smiled, casting a covert glance at Dervan as she did so.

Talia guessed this was her sister's way of getting back at Dervan, showing him she did not care. The trouble was Paul would now be the one to get hurt. He really had got it badly where Serine was concerned!

When the two men had left Talia tried to reason with Serine. 'It won't work, you know, playing Paul off against Dervan. It won't make Dervan jealous. It's all over between you.'

'And you would know, I suppose?' snapped Serine. 'He's confided in you?'

Talia sighed. 'I know he was never serious where you were concerned. You were the one doing all the chasing.'

'No, I was not,' denied Serine. 'He really liked me.'

'And he still does,' said Talia softly. 'But he doesn't love you. There is a difference.'

'I could make him, if he'd let me.'

Talia shook her head. 'You'd be wasting your time, and I don't think using Paul is the answer either. It's not fair on him.'

'Nothing's fair, according to you,' pouted Serine.

'Paul's too nice to be hurt.'

'I shan't hurt him.'

'The trouble with you, Serine,' said Talia softly, 'is that you don't know when you're hurting anyone. All you're interested in is getting your own way.'

'I don't think that's a bad thing,' retorted Serine. 'If you'd had your way I'd still be living at home. But I shan't come back, not ever. If I can't have Dervan then I'll find someone else. I have no intention of living in poverty for the rest of my life.'

Talia clamped her lips and went back into her office. There was no reasoning with Serine in this frame of mind.

As arranged, Paul picked Serine up that evening, and Talia was left to her own devices. She was deliberating whether to settle for a snack and a drink in the complex's bar, or go out for a proper meal, when Dervan arrived.

As always when he turned up like this she was taken completely by surprise, and stood back for him to enter. He had not spoken to her today at the office, except when necessary, and she thought he had given up on her. Nevertheless her own feelings had in no way changed and she experienced the now customary awakening of her senses. 'Would you like a drink?' she asked.

He shook his head and put his hands on her shoulders. His grip hurt, but Talia did not flinch. Then he smiled, a tender, all-encompassing smile that touched her nerve-ends and set everything jangling. 'Now that I've got Serine off my back, perhaps I can see more of you?'

Talia frowned. 'What do you mean?'

'Isn't it obvious? She's at last taken the hint. She's realised that I never intended anything serious.'

Hope flared, but died just as instantly, and she backed away from him, her grey eyes horrified. 'You've been using me! You've been using me to get rid of Serine—me and those other girls. It was all deliberate!'

'I admit I used Zoe and Claire,' Dervan smiled. 'They played along because I asked them to. I wanted to teach Serine a lesson. I wanted her to believe that she meant no more to me than any other girl I dated.'

'So why couldn't you have told me?' snapped Talia, not altogether convinced that he was speaking the truth.

'Because I was afraid you might tell Serine, and I couldn't risk that.'

'But why did you have to use me as well?'

He looked hurt. 'Talia, I didn't use you. I genuinely wanted your company. I know I should have waited until Serine had got used to the idea that there was nothing between us, but how could I when you're here for such a short time?'

Talia wanted to believe him, but couldn't. She was convinced he had no real interest in her. She intrigued him, perhaps. He wanted an affair. But he was not in love with her. And there was no point in settling for anything less.

'I'm sorry I don't share your feelings,' she said bluntly. 'I'd like you to go.'

Sudden anger flared his nostrils, but his voice when he spoke was carefully controlled. 'Are you saying that your response to me is nothing more than physical?'

She nodded. 'I told you that once before.'

'I didn't believe you.'

'Then you'd jolly well better believe it this time, because it's true.' Her cheeks coloured as she spoke and she turned away.

Dervan swiftly swung her to face him. 'I still think you're lying, Talia. What are you afraid of?' Once again his fingers bit into her shoulders.

'Why should I be afraid of anything?' she asked, bravely looking up at him.

'You're afraid of me for some reason. I've always known it, and I'd like to know why.'

'No, I'm not,' she claimed quickly, too quickly perhaps, for the glimmer of a smile curved his lips.

'Are you afraid that I might upset your nice cosy little life? You're happy doing your typing at home and keeping your house clean and tidy. Is that it? You don't want anything more adventurous?'

It wasn't that she didn't want it, she thought. She couldn't imagine anything more exciting than travelling the world with him. But not on a casual basis. Not so that he could send her packing the instant he got tired of her. But she said none of this to Dervan. 'You wouldn't understand. It's something I can't explain.'

'Then explain this,' he demanded gruffly, and before Talia had time to realise his intentions she was crushed against him, his mouth firmly on hers.

She knew she must show so sign of response, even though her whole body leapt into pulsing life. But it was hard standing still and resolute. especially when his lips moved over hers with deliberate sensuality.

She closed her eyes and told herself it meant nothing. *Nothing!* But how could she, when it meant everything? She was on the verge of giving in to him, of throwing caution to the wind and wildly returning his kiss, when he savagely pushed her from him. 'Maybe you're right,' he scorned. 'Maybe you aren't worth bothering with. It seems that yet again I've misjudged you, but you can be very sure I won't do it any more.' With that he turned and walked out of the apartment.

Talia collapsed on to the settee in tears. Why was she being so stubborn? she asked herself repeatedly. Why, when he was the only man she had ever truly loved? Why didn't she take what he was offering and make the most of it? Because, came back the simple answer, you're being wise. Letting yourself get too involved with Dervan will cause nothing but heartache.

Yet even though she knew this to be true, Talia could not stem her tears. For exactly how long she lay there she did not know. Some time later she dragged herself under the shower, then crawled into bed. When Serine returned she pretended to be asleep. There was no way she could talk to her sister.

From then until it was time for her to return to England Talia hardly spoke to Dervan. She knew, from Paul, that he had agreed to install a computer, but Dervan did not ask her again about whether she would agree to operate it, or even about joining him permanently. She was being given no chance to change her mind again.

'I think you're being unnecessarily hard on Dervan,' said Paul, when one day he managed to prise the truth from her. 'He might not turn out how you think.'

'And pigs might fly,' snapped Talia.

For once Paul's joky mood deserted him and he shook his head sadly.

Nor would she discuss Dervan with Serine. Whenever her sister tried to question her she changed the subject.

On the day of her flight she said goodbye to her sister and Paul. She had shaken hands with Dervan the day before when she left the office. His face had been a mask of indifference. Talia had no way of telling whether he was pleased to see the back of her or genuinely regretted her going.

Paul had another couple of days before his holiday finished, and by now he was very much in love with Serine, and it looked as though she had fallen for him too. Though you could never tell with Serine. Talia wouldn't have liked to lay a bet that she had given up on Dervan. The testing time would come when Paul left too. The trouble was neither of them would know what was happening.

It did not take Talia long to get back into her routine, but she was surprised at how dull she found it. Before, she had been quite happy in her work, had always felt a sense of achievement. Now it was one long day's slog after another, and for what? As Dervan had said, the money was nothing for the hours she put in.

It came as quite a surprise when Paul visited her just before Christmas. When she opened her front door and saw his grinning face she was too shocked for words.

'Come on,' he said, 'don't say you're not pleased to see me.'

'How did you know where I lived?' gasped Talia.

'Serine told me. How are you, Talia? How you are coping? Not very well, by the look of you.'

'Come in,' she said. 'I'll make you a cup of tea.'

He followed her into the kitchen, leaning against a cupboard as she busied herself filling the kettle. 'Still pining for Dervan?'

She shrugged and looked wistful. 'I can't help it.'

'You could always go back.'

'No!' She almost shouted the word. 'I have my pride.'

'What is it they say, pride always goes before a fall? Pick yourself up, Talia. Do it before it's too late.'

Talia frowned. 'What do you mean, too late? He hasn't got anyone else, has he?'

Paul held up his hand soothingly. 'Not as far as I know, but there are always plenty of girls on the lookout for a rich husband.'

'I'm not after a rich husband. I'd marry Dervan if he were penniless.'

'Perhaps you should have told him that,' said Paul softly.

'How could I, when he never said anything about loving me?' Talia flashed.

'Perhaps he was waiting to see how you felt?' asked Paul.

Talia shook her head wildly. 'I don't think so. Let's not talk about Dervan. How about you—you and Serine? She hardly ever writes to me.'

His grin returned. 'I'm hoping to marry her. I'm saving hard to go out there again, and when I do I shall pop the question.'

'Oh, Paul, I'm so pleased! I can't believe Serine's fallen in love with you. She always wanted—well, you know what she wanted.'

'A rich guy? I know. But I think I managed to persuade her that money isn't everything.'

'If you did that, you're a genius,' she said admiringly. 'I hope you don't find you've let yourself in for something you can't handle.'

'I don't think so,' he replied confidently.

A few days later she had a phone call from Serine. 'What's wrong?' Talia asked at once. It was unlike Serine to phone just to say hello.

'I want you to do me a favour,' her sister said without preamble. 'I'm going to get married, and I want you to tell Paul.'

Talia went numb. Her heart stopped beating, then began again at twice its normal rate. She clutched the phone like a lifeline. It was Dervan. It had to be. There hadn't been time for Serine to get close to anyone else. Oh, God, she wanted to die! How could she face meeting him as her brother-in-law? She couldn't. She simply couldn't.

'Who—who is it?' she croaked. 'Who is this man you're going to marry?'

CHAPTER SEVEN

'Talia, I can't hear you. Are you still there?' Serine's voice came clearly down the telephone line.

'Yes, I'm here. I said—who are you—marrying?' She did not want to hear Dervan's name, but it was a question she must ask.

'No one you know,' came Serine's cheerful response. 'His name's Emilio. He owns a chain of boutiques throughout the islands here. He's fabulously wealthy.'

Talia sat down. The relief was so great that it weakened her limbs. 'Oh, Serine, not someone else! What's he like? How old is he?' But she was not really interested at this moment. All she could think about was that it wasn't Dervan.

Serine chatted about her new boyfriend

for several more minutes, then asked Talia again if she would tell Paul.

'I think,' said Talia slowly, 'that you should tell him yourself. You owe him that at least.' And she gently put down the phone.

She wondered whether she ought to go out to Lanzarote again and see what sort of a man it was Serine had got herself tangled with this time. Then she remembered Dervan's warning to stop mothering her. He was right. Let Serine make a few mistakes. It was the only way she would learn.

Several days passed before she saw Paul again, and when he turned up Talia knew Serine had not told him. He was still walking on air, still making plans, telling Talia how much he loved her sister.

Talia was undecided what to do. Tell Paul, or let him find out for himself? But she couldn't do that. It wouldn't be fair.

'Have you heard from Serine lately?' he

asked, giving her the opening she needed. 'She never answered my last two letters. I hope she's all right.'

'Actually,' said Talia slowly, 'she rang me the other day.'

'She did?' His face lit up again. 'What did she say?'

Her lips twisted ruefully as she chose her words. 'I'm sorry, Paul, she's—well—oh, I don't want to tell you this, but—it's all over between you. She's—found someone else.'

His face froze. He just stared and stared at her. No emotion, nothing.

'Paul, I'm sorry. But you did know what she was like.'

'Yes, I knew,' he said quietly. 'But I really thought she'd fallen in love with me.'

'And I hoped she had too. I'd like you to be my brother-in-law.'

He looked close to tears, and Talia poured him a Scotch which he downed in one swallow. 'I'll have to go and see her,' he said eventually. 'It might be because she's missing me. Serine's the type who always needs a man around her. Once she sees me again she'll realise it's me she loves and everything will be all right.' He smiled as he solved his problem. 'I'm going now, Talia. I'm going to book my ticket. You'll see, all will work out well.'

In the hall Talia put her arms around him and gave him the comfort he needed. 'I'll keep my fingers crossed, Paul.' But she didn't hold out much hope.

She opened the front door—and had the shock of her life when she saw Dervan standing there. She hadn't even realised anyone had come up her path. And she knew he would have seen them through the patterned glass.

Paul squeezed her hand and gave an encouraging smile. 'Attagirl,' he said quietly.

Dervan gave Paul no more than a curt nod as he walked past him, nor was his expression encouraging when he looked at Talia.

She knew what he must be thinking, and she cursed fate that he had chosen this precise moment to visit her. He was the last man on earth she had expected to see, but the most welcome, although he would never know that. Why had he come? He looked strained, his face thinner than she remembered, and she wondered if he was doing too much.

'May I come in?' he asked. 'Or is that pleasure reserved for Paul?' The hardness in his tone told Talia that, whatever his reason for being here, it was not a happy one. Unless his bitterness now was purely because he had caught her in Paul's arms? Maybe he had come to make his peace with her? The thought brought fresh hope, and her heart panicked.

'I'm sorry, of course, yes,' she said. and stepped back for him to enter. Every nerve-end tingled as he brushed by her, renewing all the emotions and feelings she had tried her hardest to forget these last weeks.

She led him through into her sitting-room, and was glad she had just polished. It smelled of lavender and looked cosy, despite the old furniture. The chairs were worn, she knew, and desperately needed replacing, but there was never enough money for things like that, so she had covered them in chintz and kept the covers clean and neat.

Dervan looked around before taking a seat near the fireplace. There was no fire, because she had central heating, but even that was turned down low. Talia was always cost-conscious.

'Can I get you a drink?' she asked. 'A Scotch, perhaps?'

He glanced at Paul's empty glass on the table, and she could only surmise what he was thinking. 'I'll have a cup of coffee,' he said. 'Black, no sugar.'

'Yes, I remember,' answered Talia quietly. 'I won't be a minute. Would you like the television on?'

He shook his head. 'I'll sit here with my thoughts.'

In the kitchen her mind was in a turmoil. It was impossible to guess why he was here. To call a truce? Again the happy thought ran through her mind. To tell her about Serine? *Serine!* That was it. *Something was wrong.* She rushed back into the sitting-room. 'Is Serine all right? Is that why you're here? Is she ill?'

'Serine is perfectly well,' Dervan announced calmly.

'Oh—good,' she said, and returned to the kitchen. The kettle boiled and she made two cups of coffee, adding milk and sugar to her own. She took them through on a tray with a plate of home-made shortbread.

Dervan's head was resting back on the chair, his eyes closed, and for just a second she was able to observe him. He really did look drawn, almost haggard, and she wondered if it were he who wasn't well.

But in that case he wouldn't be here, surely?

Talia put the tray down and he opened his eyes. 'How involved are you with Paul?'

The directness of his question startled her and she settled into a chair the other side of the fireplace before answering. 'I'm not.'

His eyes narrowed. 'It didn't look that way to me.'

'I hardly ever see him. He calls in occasionally to talk about Serine.'

'Is that what you were doing when I saw you—talking?'

He sounded condemning, and Talia's eyes blazed with sudden fury. 'What I was doing was my affair. Perhaps you'd like to get to the real point of your visit?'

'Very well, we'll forget Paul—for the moment. It's Serine I'm concerned about.'

'You said she was well,' cut in Talia with a frown.

'So she is. But I'm afraid I'm not

happy about the company she's keeping. I think you ought to come back with me to Lanzarote and have a word with her.'

'You're talking about Emilio?'

He frowned. 'You know?'

Talia nodded. 'Serine phoned me. What's he like?'

'Not a man to be trusted. Forty if he's a day. Unscrupulous. Noted for his affairs with nubile young girls.'

'Serine says he's going to marry her.'

'Not a hope. He says that to them all, then keeps them happy when the affair's over by giving them expensive pieces of jewellery.'

Talia began to feel really alarmed. Up until now Serine's affairs had been harmless flirtations. She had never been in any real danger, even from Dervan—although Talia had not known that at the time she'd gone shooting off to Lanzarote. But it was ironic, Dervan coming here now to tell her to have a word with Serine.

She eyed him boldly. 'I thought I was

supposed to be leaving her to get on with her own life. Wasn't that what you advised? Wasn't I protecting her too much?'

A muscle jerked in his jaw. 'Point taken, Talia, but I hadn't realised she'd do something like this.'

'Now you can see why I've always kept a tight rein on her?'

He nodded.

'Is that really why you're here? Couldn't you have phoned?' She waited to hear him say it was an excuse to see her.

'I had business in England. It was an ideal opportunity, killing two birds with one stone, so to speak.'

Talia slumped in her chair, not realising the sudden dejection that had come over her face.

Dervan eyed her thoughtfully, but all he said was, 'If you can get yourself organised by tomorrow you can fly back with me.'

'Impossible,' said Talia sharply. 'I have too much to do.'

His thick brows lifted sardonically. 'Still

hammering away at your typewriter?'

'Of course, it's my living.'

'How long will it take you to finish the work you have on hand?'

She shrugged. 'I don't know. A couple of days, perhaps. Three at the most, if nothing else comes in.'

'Then I'll wait. And you can tell your customers that you won't be doing this sort of thing any longer.'

Talia gasped. 'I will not! I need the money. And it happens to be more flexible working this way, which suits me very well.'

'I can find you a much better job, more highly paid, more suited to your skills.'

'In Lanzarote?' she asked suspiciously.

'Well, yes, I still need a computer operator, but I didn't actually mean that. I was talking about my office in the West End. They have a vacancy, if you're interested. I'm over here to conduct interviews.'

'No, thanks,' said Talia, her tone clipped.

He did not look disappointed, which made her think that he had made up the offer on the spur of the moment just to see what her reaction would be. She was glad she had said no.

He picked up his coffee and after taking a sip cradled the cup in his hands. Brown hands, long-fingered, well manicured. Talia wished it were her they were holding so closely.

'Would you like a piece of shortbread?' she asked abruptly, offering him the plate. She mustn't think things like that. It was insanity.

Dervan shook his head.

Talia put the plate down and took a biscuit herself, nibbling it absent-mindedly.

'Tell me more about you and Paul,' he said all of a sudden.

She shot him a savage glance. 'What would you like to hear, that we're lovers?'

'Are you?' His eyes locked into hers, as

they had so many times before, and Talia could not deny the sudden racing of her pulses. It was as though he was trying to look right into her mind.

'Of course we're damn well not. We never have been and we're never likely to be.'

'Then why were you in his arms?'

'What a suspicious mind you have!' she spat coldly. 'I was comforting him, if you must know. I'd just told him about Serine and Emilio.'

'Ah! I wondered whether he knew. He was smitten with her himself at one time, I believe?'

'More than that. He planned to ask her to marry him. He was really knocked for six.'

'I can imagine.' His black brows rose smoothly. 'What's he going to do about it?'

'What can he do?' demanded Talia. 'I've never known Serine take up again with one of her ex-boyfriends.'

'Have you told Paul this?'

'No, of course not. I couldn't shatter him completely. He's talking about going to see her and I hope he does. I think he could do more good than me.'

'Then you won't be joining me on my return flight?'

She thought he looked disappointed, then decided she had imagined it. 'I don't see the point. Serine's got past the age of listening to me.'

'Then I'm wasting my time sitting here.' He finished his coffee and stood up.

Talia's heart dipped low into her shoes. She wanted him to stay, she wanted to talk to him, look at him, hold him. Oh, God, how she wanted him! Her love for him was as strong as ever. What could she say to keep him here a while longer?

He said it for her. 'I'll call back tomorrow to see if you've changed your mind. Unless you'd like to have dinner with me tonight?'

Yes, yes, a thousand times, yes! her

heart clamoured. More sedately, she found herself saying, 'That would be nice. Thank you, Dervan.'

'I'll pick you up at eight.'

'I'll be ready.' She would be ready at seven, at six. As soon as he had gone.

Dervan nodded a brief goodbye and walked down the path without looking round once. But Talia did not mind. She was bursting with happiness. Dervan turning up was something she had dreamed about but never expected. Already her mind was racing ahead, planning what she was going to wear. The only thing marring her pleasure was Serine and Emilio. But Paul would sort them out, she felt sure. In any case, she was not going to let thoughts of her sister spoil her enjoyment this evening.

She chose a brown and cream knitted dress which hung in flattering pleats. It had a round neck and full sleeves gathered into a tight cuff. With a gold chain and gold earrings it looked perfect for wherever he might take her. It was one of her better dresses, bought in a moment of madness, but now she was glad she had something that would not let her down.

Dervan arrived on the dot of eight and studied her carefully, but made no comment. Talia didn't care. He didn't have to. Just being with him was sufficient. She felt as if she had been born again. The weeks of sadness were forgotten; she was alive, startlingly alive. Vibrant and happy and walking on air.

He was wearing a navy lounge suit with a blue silk shirt and maroon tie, and he looked good. She feasted her eyes on him and couldn't drag them away when they met his. It was a meeting of souls. Or was it? Did he feel the same way as she did? Was that the reason for his visit? Was all the rest of it an excuse? She wished she knew. She wished with all her heart that she knew what was going on in his mind.

'Let's go,' he said, breaking the spell.

The evening was not the success Talia had hoped it would be. Dervan excited her, yes, and his eyes were on her often, accelerating her pulses, making her toy with her food instead of eating it. But there were no intimacies. He spoke of Serine, he spoke of his work, and the computer system Paul's company was installing. He even said that he planned to see Paul about it before he returned to Lanzarote. But he never spoke about themselves, and he never touched her or even hinted that he was still interested in any sort of relationship with her, no matter how platonic.

By the end of the evening Talia had begun to despair, though what she had hoped for she was not sure. She thought that, as he had taken the trouble to come to see her, he must feel something, that he had used her sister as an excuse. But she now realised it was all wishful thinking. He had no more interest in her than he had in Serine.

He took her home and she wondered whether to ask him in for a drink, whether to prolong their time together, prolong the agony; or let him walk out of her life. Again he took the decision away from her.

'Goodnight, Talia.' He took her face firmly between his hands, looked deeply into her eyes, then kissed her. It was a kiss that started off as a friendly gesture and ended in a passionate embrace.

All the feelings that Talia had kept tightly reined burst free. It was impossible to control them. She had dreamt of this moment for so long, had imagined kissing Dervan so many times, that reality was but a culmination of these fantasies, and she responded without conscious thought.

Her lips parted. She gave tiny animal whimpers and wrapped her arms around him, straining close, aching with her love for him, wanting this moment to go on and on.

'Let's go inside, Talia.' He sounded as desperate as she.

After fumbling for her key Talia finally managed to open the door, and once it was closed behind them they fell into each other's arms. She did not stop to think about the rightness or the wrongness of the situation, merely taking what was being offered, accepting it, needing it, wanting it. It had been so long. God, how she wanted him!

He too was hungry for her. His kisses became more and more demanding. His hands roved her body, exploring the rounded contours of her breasts, sending fresh shudders of desire through her. 'Talia!' he breathed.

'Dervan?' It was a whimper, a question. What did he want of her?

The next moment they were through into her sitting-room. He unbuckled her belt and began pulling her dress over her head. It was an awkward dress to get off, but he was adept and in the briefest space of time it was lying on a chair and he was removing her cream lace bra.

Clad in nothing but her briefs, Talia felt an instant of shyness, especially when he looked at her for several long seconds. 'Beautiful,' he murmured, 'absolutely beautiful.'

Then they came together, and his kisses now pulsed over her delicately perfumed skin. Her breasts tingled and hardened when his mouth and tongue slowly and torturingly nibbled and kissed every inch. She held his head, she watched him, she shuddered as wave after wave of pure animal hunger washed over her, and finally she let out a cry of sheer ecstatic abandonment when he took her nipple into his mouth. It was an experience to beat all experiences.

When he finally lifted his head his eyes were glazed, his mouth wet and soft and she touched his lips with a questioning finger.

'That's what I came for,' he said. 'That and more of it. I've not been able to get you out of my mind, Talia. Have you any idea what you do to me?'

She nodded, her own eyes as filled with emotion as his. But even as she craved fulfilment she was afraid. She had denied him in Lanzarote, and he was a man used to getting his own way. Was he after nothing more than an affair? How would she ever know, when he spoke not one word of love? He wanted her, he desired her, he craved her, he hungered for her, but did he love her? These feelings alone were not enough.

But for the moment she did not tell him what she was thinking. Her body craved his with equal intensity, and when he pulled her against him she yielded her soft warmth to his.

'Talia, oh, Talia! The nights I've lain awake wanting you in my arms!' He nuzzled her neck, her ears, the corners of her mouth, and his long, hard body confirmed his need.

'I've thought of you too,' she whispered huskily. 'Many times. But I don't—'

His mouth on hers quelled the protest she was about to utter. 'My Talia!' he breathed. One hand cradled her head, the other moved lower, feeling the shape of her, the warmth, the quivers of emotion. He felt her waist, her hips, her stomach, his fingers inching inside the flimsy material of her briefs.

'No, Dervan.' She regretted the protest, but knew it must be said.

He stopped instantly and a tiny frown lined his brow. 'Don't be afraid, Talia. I won't hurt you.'

'I know.' Her own face was creased in anguish. 'But I don't want to—to go any further. I'm not—I can't—'

He stifled her cries with a kiss. A gentle, persuasive, devastating kiss. A kiss that sent fresh rivers of fire through her limbs and an aching need that would take for ever to die. 'You want me as much as I want you. Isn't that right?'

She nodded, her eyes pained.

'So why stop me? Why punish yourself?'

Because I love you and you don't love me. It wouldn't be right. It would be sex for the sake of sex, and I don't want that. She shook her head, tears in her eyes now. 'I can't expect you to understand.'

'You could try me.'

Again she shook her head and the lump in her throat threatened to choke her.

Dervan's face grew serious. There was a sudden minute's silence when they did nothing except look at each other. Then he said softly, 'Talia, will you marry me?'

Whatever Talia had been expecting, it was not this, but she knew instantly why he had said it and her blood boiled. 'Damn you, Dervan! Is this the only way you can think of getting me into your bed?'

A frown carved his forehead. 'Talia, I—'

She would not let him finish. 'Get out!' She snatched up her dress and tugged it over her head, her eyes glaring at him.

'I didn't mean—'

'I said, *get out!*'

'Talia, please!'

She marched to the door and held it open, her whole body rigid with anger, her chin high, her eyes watching him like a hawk.

'I'll come and see you again when you've cooled down,' he said, pausing in front of her.

'You'd better not,' she snapped. 'You're not welcome in my house again!'

His eyes were sad and he looked even more haggard than before, but Talia hardened her heart He was a swine. He was a con man. He was trying to trick her. He was. *He was!*

When he had gone the tears raced down her cheeks. She closed the door and slumped against the wall. The tears turned to sobs. But she knew she had done the right thing.

Eventually Talia crawled up to bed, but she lay awake for long, painful hours, refusing to believe that Dervan's reason for proposing was anything other than devious, and the more she thought about it, the angrier she grew.

The phone rang early the next morning, too early for it to be one of her customers, and she knew it was Dervan. Her heart slammed against her ribcage as she answered, then died a quick death when she heard Paul's voice.

'Good morning, Talia. Have you anything exciting to tell me?'

'If you're talking about Dervan, no,' she said abruptly.

'Things didn't go too well, eh?' He sounded surprised. 'A pity. I thought he might have come to whisk you back to his love-nest in Lanzarote.'

Talia grimaced into the receiver. 'Actually, he did suggest it. He even threw in an offer of marriage.' Her tone was caustic. 'But I refused.'

'What?'

'You heard,' she laughed.

'But why, when you love him? Isn't that what you wanted?'

'All he was interested in was getting his own way,' she protested. 'He took me out to dinner, we kissed, he wanted to make love, I refused. Hence the proposal. Get the picture?'

'But, Talia—' Paul sounded flabbergasted, 'no man in his right mind would suggest marriage simply because he wanted to make love to a girl. You must have it wrong.'

'No, I haven't,' she snapped, though she knew she was behaving unreasonably. Paul was right. But on the other hand, what possible reason had Dervan got for asking her to marry him? He didn't love her. So why? She needed to know.

'I take it you're not seeing him again?'

'I don't want to, but he said he'd be in touch once I'd had time to cool down.'

'You actually told him what you thought?' he asked in amazement

'Why not?' she defended.

'Oh, Talia!'

'I don't care. And by the way, he said

he'd be coming to see you about his new computer.'

'Did he say anything about Serine?'

Talia guessed this was the real reason Paul had telephoned. 'Yes, he's worried about her. He doesn't approve of Emilio, says he's too old. I think you should definitely go to see her, Paul.'

'You bet I will,' he said firmly. 'I've already booked my flight for tomorrow. Oh, heavens, is that the time? I must go. Chin up, Talia. Things are not always what they seem.'

It was easy for him to say that she thought as she busied herself making breakfast; he didn't know what Dervan was really like.

Talia typed fast and furiously throughout the day, getting through an enormous amount of work, trying to push him out of her mind, starting every time the phone rang, almost afraid to answer, but it was never Dervan.

She had almost convinced herself that he

had been bluffing, that he had no intention of coming to see her again, when the doorbell rang. She glanced at her watch. Seven o'clock. She had not realised it was so late.

In the hall she could see at a glance that it was Dervan, impatiently moving from foot to foot, his hand hovering over the bell-push ready to ring again. Talia was tempted to pretend she was out, but she knew it would get her nowhere. He would come back again.

When she opened the door her expression was anything but welcoming, and she stood and waited to hear what he had got to say. She had no intention of asking him in.

'Hello, Talia.' His eyes narrowed as he tried to calculate the depth of her hostility.

'You're wasting your time,' she said bluntly. 'I've not changed my opinion of you.' Nor had her body stopped responding to his magnetism. It was still there, as strong as ever. Damn the man!

'I've been to see Paul.'

Her grey eyes widened and she hoped Paul hadn't said anything.

'He can't go to Lanzarote after all.'

A suspicious frown creased her brow. 'You've told him not to go, it that it? You're still trying to get me out there?'

'Paul's decision was his own,' he returned crisply. 'Something urgent cropped up that only he can take care of.'

'I don't believe you.'

He shrugged. 'Ring him.'

'I will. Is that all you came to tell me?'

'I came to insist that you fly out to Serine,' Dervan said impatiently. 'She's heading for big trouble.'

Talia eyed him solidly for a full half-minute, fighting a battle with her conscience and her heart. 'I'll come,' she said at last, 'on the understanding that you keep out of my way.' It crucified her saying this, but what else could she do? If they spent too much time together she would submit to the magnetism that had attracted her right from the very beginning.

'I can't promise that, Talia.'

'Why not?'

'Because I meant what I said last night and I shall do my very best to get you to change your mind.'

Talia realised he had her cornered, but she could not ignore Serine's dilemma, even if it meant a load of trouble for herself. She eyed him belligerently. 'I suppose you win.'

His smile was triumphant. 'I knew I would. Be ready tomorrow at noon. We're leaving then.'

'But—'

She was given no chance to protest. He had already turned and was walking down the path. Short of racing after him and arguing in the middle of the road, Talia had no recourse but to accept his decision.

She phoned Paul and he confirmed what Dervan had told her. 'I'm sick as a pig about the whole thing,' he said, 'but there's nothing I can do. You will talk to Serine? You will tell her how I feel? And that I'll be out there as soon as I possibly can? I love her so much, Talia. I don't want to lose her.'

'I'll do my best,' she promised.

Talia spent the rest of the evening finishing off her typing and ringing her customers. They were not very pleased that she was going away again, and she could see herself losing their business.

By eleven the next morning she was ready, and promptly at twelve Dervan arrived. He was dressed very casually in fawn trousers and shirt with a brown cashmere sweater, and a brown leather jacket. Her pulses quickened at the mere sight of him, though she carefully schooled her feelings. She had made up her mind that there would be no recurrence of the other night.

Yet even as his eyes locked into hers she knew it would be impossible. He was doing it to her already, and what was more maddening was that he knew it. His smile was slow and warm. 'I'm glad you're ready, Talia. Shall we go?'

She nodded, but it seemed an age before he looked away, and by this time her heart was beating frantically. 'I'll have a final check around the house while you put my case in your car,' she said. It wasn't really necessary, she'd checked it a dozen times, but she needed a few minutes' breathing space.

When she finally joined Dervan in his car she had herself under control, and during the short drive to the airport they talked generally about the state of the country and the weather and all the usual topics of conversation between two people who had only just met.

Talia hated the tension between them and knew it was of her own making, but how else could she behave? If only he would say, 'Talia, I love you.' Then everything would be all right.

At least on the plane there would be other people around them, there would not be this intimacy that was so difficult to avoid. But again she was thwarted. Talia could not believe her eyes when Dervan led her towards the executive lounge and then out to a Lear jet.

He laughed at her puzzled expression. 'Quicker than waiting for a scheduled flight.'

She swallowed hard. 'Do you fly this thing yourself?'

'No, indeed. It has its own pilot. Come and meet him.'

Was there to be no escape? thought Talia. For however many hours it would take them to fly to Lanzarote, she and Dervan were the only passengers. There was no way now she could avoid him. He had had it planned all along.

CHAPTER EIGHT

Inside the plane it was as cosy as Talia had feared. There were armchairs, rather than normal seats, a video and an audio unit and a bar stocked with every conceivable drink.

'Pretty impressive, don't you think?' Dervan asked with a grin.

Talia nodded. 'Is it yours?'

'Chartered,' he replied, 'but I use it so often I'm thinking of buying one.'

Once they were airborne he asked her what she would like to drink.

'A gin and tonic, please,' she answered, 'a large one.'

An eyebrow quirked. 'Is it that bad?'

'I never expected to be quite so alone with you,' she said bluntly.

'And you can't handle it?'

'I didn't say that,' she returned sharply.

'Good.' He looked as though he was having difficulty in suppressing a smile. 'I'm looking forward to some time spent together.'

He busied himself making her drink pouring the same for himself, then sitting down, the ankle of one leg resting on the knee of his other, totally relaxed.

Talia, on the other hand, sat on the edge of her seat, her ankles crossed neatly, her drink in her hand.

'You look at though you're ready to take flight at any minute!' Then he grinned as he realised what he had said. 'No pun intended. Sit back, Talia, I'm not going to eat you.'

Grudgingly she moved back in her seat allowing its soft comfort to swallow her up.

They sat in silence for a few moments, then he said quietly, 'Why won't you marry me, Talia?'

She had not expected such a blunt

question, at least not so soon, and for a second did not know what to say. She merely looked at him with a pained expression in her eyes.

'You said I wouldn't understand why you stopped me making love to you,' he went on, his eyes never leaving her face. He seemed to be looking deep inside her, turning her stomach over, causing every nerve-end to tremble into life. 'I'm sure I will. Why don't you try me?'

Talia ran the tip of her tongue over her suddenly dry lips. Her heart was pounding so hard that it hurt. 'I'd rather not.'

'Is it so difficult?'

'It's deeply personal,' she said quietly.

'And I don't deserve to hear, even though you know I want to marry you?'

'Your reasons for asking me are not the right ones,' she said flatly, taking a sip of her drink and trying to avoid his eyes. But it was not easy. They were hypnotic. No matter how many times she looked away, she was always drawn back to him. And he never stopped looking at her.

'Do you still think I suggested it so that I could make love to you?'

Talia grimaced. 'I'm sorry I said that. It was stupid.'

'I'm glad you realise it.'

'But that doesn't stop me from thinking that you have some other ulterior motive,' she said sharply.

Dervan's black brows drew together. 'Such as?'

'I don't know. But it was a strange proposal, you must admit.'

'Why? Because I didn't get down on my knees and declare undying love?'

'It would be nice to hear that you love me,' she said huskily.

His frown deepened. 'Are you suggesting that those three words, "I love you", would make all the difference? Words are easy, Talia. But they don't always mean anything.' He sounded suddenly bitter. 'Can't you tell how I feel about you? Haven't I shown you?'

Talia bit her lip nervously, then decided this was a time for honesty. 'You've shown me that you desire me in a sexual manner. But marrying a person means more than that. It's friendship, and understanding, and sharing, and a host of other things.'

'All of which I can give you.'

Talia shook her head. 'No. You're saying that because I've put the words into your head. It has to be voluntary. It needed to come from you in the first place. Please let's drop the subject, Dervan. I don't wish to discuss it any more.'

'For the moment,' he agreed, not looking very pleased, but accepting that she was upset.

He slotted a cassette into the tape-recorder and they listened to Neil Diamond singing, 'The story of my life'. It couldn't have been deliberate, and yet it was as though Dervan was using the words to tell her something.

And all the time it was playing he watched her, those deeply sensuous eyes sending unspoken messages, turning her into a seething mass of sensation.

None of the other songs after that were as potent but the damage was done. Talia felt all woman. She had accused Dervan of wanting her, but at this moment it was she who wanted him. Badly. If he had stood up and taken her into his arms she would have given in to him without a moment's hesitation.

Instead he suggested they ate. He miraculously produced steaming hot ready-prepared dinners and Talia tucked into croquette potatoes, peas, carrots and stewed beef. It was delicious. Afterwards came raspberry mousse and cheese and biscuits, and finally strong, aromatic coffee.

They sat at a tiny table, their knees almost touching, and it was the most intimate meal Talia had ever had. Or was it because of her mood? There were no candles or soft music. The tape had stopped and Dervan hadn't bothered to replace it. There was just the noise of the engine. Apart from that nothing. Silence. The two of them together. Dervan spoke occasionally, and she answered, their tones hushed, almost as though they were in a sacred place. Neil Diamond's song had cast a spell over her, or was it Dervan?

There was something different about him. He was relaxed; the perpetual frown lines had almost gone from his forehead. He was gentle. He was attentive, passing her the salt when it was but a thought in her head. A napkin? It was there. She dropped her fork; a clean one appeared. Her wine-glass was refilled. Her love for him welled and welled, threatening to overspill and reveal itself. If he was trying to prove that he cared for her then he was certainly going the right way about it!

Afterwards they resumed their seats in the armchairs, and although neither spoke for a while it was not an uncomfortable silence. For almost the first time Talia felt at ease with him. He had slotted in another cassette, not a vocal this time, but soft relaxing music.

She closed her eyes and was almost asleep when he said, 'I want to tell you something, Talia, something that's very difficult for me to speak about, but I think you should know.'

A faint frown creased her brow. 'You don't have to, Dervan. Not if it's—'

'I want to,' he insisted.

She nodded and sat with her hands folded in her lap, waiting for him to start.

'When I was eighteen I met a girl and fell in love. I loved her more than life itself, and I wanted us to get married.' He looked down at his hands as he spoke, pausing, as though transporting himself back in time. 'Our parents thought we were too young, so, at their insistence, we waited. We didn't mind. We both knew our love would stand the test of time. I was twenty-two when we finally fixed a date.' Another pause, and this time when he spoke again his voice was barely audible.

'A week before the wedding, she died.'

'Oh, Dervan, that's awful!' exclaimed Talia, deeply shocked. 'You must have been devastated.'

'I was. A drunken driver killed her.' His fingers curled into his palms as he spoke, and Talia could see that he was deeply moved, even after all this time.

'I knew I would never fall in love again, but I did, years later. Again I lost her.' He gave a soft snort of anger. 'She didn't die this time, she walked out on me—and again the wedding was fixed. I don't know why. I thought she loved me; she said she did. And I loved her. I always believed in being totally honest where emotions were concerned. I never stopped telling her how much I cared for her. It seems,' he went on bitterly, 'that I'm destined always to lose the ones I love.'

'So you're determined never to fall in love again?' she asked softly. His confession had deeply moved her and gave her some insight into the way his mind worked.

He stood up and walked the length of the cabin and back again. 'To be brutally frank, Talia, I'm afraid to. And I wouldn't admit that to anyone else.'

'I think it was simply bad luck,' she said. 'I don't think you should be afraid. It can't happen a third time.'

'No?' he asked harshly. 'Don't they say things happen in threes?'

'I'm not superstitious,' she said. 'And I can't believe you are.'

'Perhaps not,' he shrugged, 'but you must admit I haven't had a very good deal out of life.'

'So you want to marry me without love?' she asked, unaware that her hurt was showing in her eyes. 'Isn't that a desperate measure?'

'You might see it that way,' Dervan said tersely. 'I don't.'

'How do you see it, then?'

'I want to get married, Talia. I want a son while I'm still young enough to enjoy his company.'

She frowned harshly. 'In other words, you want to use me as a baby machine?'

He winced at her bluntness. 'I wouldn't put it that crudely, Talia.'

'But it's true, isn't it?' she insisted.

'No, it's damn well not true!' he snarled. 'I like you—I like you a lot. I think we'd get on well together.'

'I don't happen to think liking a person is sufficient basis for a marriage,' she retorted. 'What would happen to the child, supposing we had one, if it didn't work out? It wouldn't be fair. No, Dervan, I can't do it.'

'I'd make damn sure it worked,' he said.

'No person can be that sure. My answer's still no.'

He sat down and his head hung low on his chest. He looked defeated, and Talia wanted to go to him and say, yes, she would marry him. She loved him and she didn't care if he did not love her. He would, in time, when he realised she was a permanent part of his life, when he realised that she had no intention of ever, ever leaving him.

But she said none of these things. It was foolish marrying a man who wanted her for purely selfish reasons. A bed-mate, a mother to his child, a housekeeper. And he would probably insist that she stay at home and look after their child, or even children, while he went away on his travels. Had he really any idea what he was asking of her? She couldn't do it. She wouldn't.

When Dervan eventually lifted his head a mask had fallen over his face. He looked at her, but there was none of that sensuality she had grown so used to in his eyes. She might have been a complete stranger. 'Is that your final decision, Talia?'

She swallowed hard and nodded.

He nodded too, as though accepting it. Then he got up and poured himself a Scotch, emptying the glass in one swallow, refilling it, and this time bringing it back to his chair.

The silence now was uncomfortable, and Talia wondered how much longer the flight would last. She closed her eyes and pretended to go to sleep, but all the time she was acutely aware of Dervan sitting opposite.

'Talia.' His brusque tone made her eyes jerk open. 'You have enough to worry about with your sister; let's forget I ever said anything. I thought it might help, but instead I appear to have made matters worse. I apologise.'

'Please, you don't have to,' she said, knowing how much this must have cost him. 'But I would like to be friends.'

His smile was so faint as to be scarcely noticeable. He took another sip of whisky and glanced at his watch. 'Another hour and we'll be there. Serine will be surprised to see you.'

'She had no idea you'd come to fetch me?'

'I didn't come for that specific reason, Talia.'

'But I'm sure she must have known you'd tell me.' And then, as a sudden thought struck her, 'My God, Dervan, I hope she hasn't got married while you've been away! It would crucify Paul.'

'He'll survive,' snapped Dervan, and it was obvious to Talia now that he was thinking of the two girls he had lost. 'But I don't think she'll do anything that stupid.'

'You don't know Serine.'

'But I know Emilio. He's only playing with her.'

They continued to make small talk until the plane landed. The warm air met them as they walked across the concourse. Customs were a mere formality and soon they were in Dervan's blue Mercedes.

The sights were familiar now to Talia—the naked mountains, the long palm-lined roads, the green and white houses, old women dressed in black with straw hats, scarves tied round their necks to shield them from the biting sand whipped up by the constant winds. Men in black hats with check shirts and loose-fitting trousers, donkeys pulling ploughs, black volcanic ash everywhere.

It brought a poignant ache to her heart. She had thrown away the chance of living here with Dervan—of being his wife. Moving with him wherever he went. Bearing his children. Enjoying the physical side of marriage, even though there was no love on his part. It would be a good life. Maybe she ought to think it over? Maybe it was foolish turning him down just because he didn't love her? He liked her, he had admitted that and they were compatible physically. So what else did she want?

Talia had given no thought to where she would be staying; there had been so much on her mind that it was the last thing to worry her. But when Dervan took her straight to his villa she looked at him askance. 'Is Serine here?' she asked.

He shook his head. 'No. She's staying with a local family. She had to move out of the apartment.'

'I hope she's not living with Emilio?' asked Talia at once, her tone sharp with fear.

He smiled reassuringly. 'Of course not'

'So what am I doing here?'

'You're staying with me,' he said bluntly.

Talia's grey eyes widened. 'I don't think that's wise.'

'Don't worry, I won't touch you. You've made your point. The next move will have to come from you. Though God knows it will be hard.' These last words were muttered through his teeth and Talia was not even sure whether he intended her to hear.

But if it was hard for him it would be hell for her. This was the last place she should be staying. 'No, Dervan, I can't.'

She turned to leave, but he caught her shoulder and twisted her back into the room. 'Don't be stupid!' He was beginning to lose his patience with her. 'We're a couple of adults, not adolescents incapable of controlling our feelings.'

He was right, of course. Talia shrugged and followed him into one of the bedrooms. He stood her case at the foot of the bed, then left her. She closed the door behind him, noting as she did so that there was no lock on it.

She put away the few clothes she had brought with her, then took a shower in the en-suite bathroom, dressing again in the kingfisher-blue dress he liked so much.

When she joined him in the sitting-room he said, 'I've arranged for a local woman to come and cook dinner—I thought you might be too tired after the journey to go out.'

'But how about Serine?' she frowned. 'When am I going to see her?'

'Tomorrow at the office would be a good time, don't you think? Then you can have my backing if you need it.'

He seemed to have it all worked out, thought Talia, but she had to agree that she did not really feel like approaching Serine tonight.

The intimacy she had felt on the plane was gone. Dervan was friendly but distant and it was all her own doing, and when Talia finally went to bed she felt like weeping into her pillow.

She hardly slept. What with Dervan and Serine, her mind was in complete turmoil. But the next morning she heard him whistling as he moved about and she was glad he appeared to have got over his black mood. But it didn't help. She still had to live with the fact that he had no intention of ever falling in love, with her or anyone else. All she could do was push it from her mind and concentrate on bringing her sister to her senses. Then they would go home.

A sudden tap on the door made her jump. 'Talia, are you awake? Breakfast's almost ready.'

Was he cooking it? she wondered as she sprang out of bed. 'I won't be long,' she called, and showered and dressed in record time.

Dervan smiled warmly when she joined him, as though yesterday's confession had never been made. 'Good morning, Talia.' Then he frowned faintly. 'You look as if you've had a bad night?'

'Thanks for nothing,' she quipped, wishing he had given her time to put on some make-up to hide the dark shadows beneath her eyes. 'It was just the strange bed, that's all. Tonight I'll sleep like a log, I promise you.'

Dervan did not look as though he believed her, and in contrast he was clear-eyed and fresh and vital—and oh, how she loved him!

He set a plate of bacon and egg, tomatoes and mushrooms in front of her. 'You can't beat a traditional English breakfast. Eat that and you'll be able to face whatever the day has to offer.'

'Do you always cook breakfast?' she asked.

He grimaced. 'Actually, no. It's often a cup of black coffee and nothing else.'

'Then I thank you,' she said demurely.

He joined her at the table that was laid with a sunny yellow cloth and yellow and white crockery. It was a very cheerful start to the morning and Talia felt immediately better.

'I don't imagine Serine will take kindly to me interfering again,' she said as she chewed a piece of perfectly cooked bacon. 'I'm afraid you might have quite a scene on your hands.'

Dervan shrugged. 'If it makes your sister see sense then it will be worth it.'

'Have you tried talking to her yourself?'

'A couple of times,' he admitted, 'but it's difficult when I've been so close. It comes across as sour grapes.'

Talia could see that but she wished Serine had listened to him. She was not looking forward to this morning at all.

On the other hand, if Serine had taken notice of what Dervan said, then he would have had no need to come and see her in England. Perhaps in effect Serine had done her a favour? Even if things weren't working out as she would have liked.

After breakfast Talia washed up and Dervan dried. It was a cosy, domesticated scene, and it broke Talia's heart. He gave no indication that they had been talking about marriage the day before. He treated her as though she were a platonic friend, or even a sister.

It was her own fault, Talia realised that. If she had taken what he offered without worrying about a little thing like love, then she would be walking on cloud nine at this moment, instead of feeling like hell.

When their hands accidentally touched as she put down a plate and he went to pick one up, it was like an electric shock. Tingles of awareness ran through her and it was all she could do to carry on as though nothing was wrong.

Dervan was once again whistling softly to himself, and it annoyed her that he was so immune. If his feelings were packed in ice then he should never have approached her in the first place. Talia slammed the next plate down so viciously that it broke.

An immediate apology sprang to her lips, but he took the washing-up cloth out of her hand and told her to go and get ready to leave. 'I'll finish here,' he said.

Tears filled her eyes as she looked at him. Did he know? Was he aware that it was because she couldn't stand the strain of loving him when he didn't love her?

In her bedroom Talia let the tears flow, and she was glad at that moment that she had not made up her eyes. But a few minutes was all it took for her to pull herself together. She had to be strong; there was no point in being otherwise.

Soon she had on her war-paint and looked, even if she did not feel it, fit to face the day—deep blue eyeshadow to match her dress, a powdering of blusher to hide her pallor, and a rose-pink lipstick to add that extra touch of colour.

Dervan eyed her closely, but there was no way of knowing what he was thinking. In his car Talia could not avoid his particularly strong brand of male magnetism. It filled the confined space so that she did nothing but breathe him in, and when he looked at her that sensualism was back in his eyes.

Talia felt as though they were bound together, united by some invisible cord. It had always been like this, and yet, because of his past experiences, Dervan was unable to unlock his heart. He could not give her what she wanted. Sex, yes. But love, no. And what good was a relationship without love?

As he drove to the office they did not speak. Words were not needed; they each knew how the other was feeling. Talia was glad when they got there. Serine had not yet arrived, but she went into her sister's room and sat down to wait. She needed a few minutes' escape from Dervan to marshal her thoughts into some sort of order.

They always started work at eight finishing at four. But eight o'clock came and went. Half-past. Nine. Half past nine. Still no sign of Serine. Talia began to worry.

She went in to Dervan's office. 'Where can Serine be?' she asked.

The frown that perpetually creased his forehead when he was working was back. 'I've no idea. She said nothing to Maria yesterday about being late. But maybe it's because she thinks I'm away.' His thick black brows rose as he waited for her to agree, but Talia knew that all he was doing was trying to placate her.

'This has something to do with Emilio, I'm sure,' she said. 'I want to know where he lives, where they both live. I want to find her.'

'I'll come with you,' said Dervan at once.

Talia shook her head. 'There's no need. There must be things here urgently needing your attention.'

But in answer he took her elbow and ushered her out of the office, calling to Maria as he did so that he would be back later in the day.

First they paid a call on the family in whose home she was staying. Dervan spoke to the woman and came back looking serious. 'Serine didn't sleep here last night,' he reported.

'Oh, no!' Talia looked at him aghast. 'Where do you think she could be?'

'Let's try Emilio,' he answered grimly.

But again they drew a blank. Emilio's office said he had gone away on a private business trip, but he had not said where, and they did not know when to expect him back. Talia was beside herself with worry. 'It's my fault—I should never have gone home and left Serine here. I should have insisted she went back with me.'

Dervan's lips were grim. 'If it's anyone's fault it's mine. I told you to lay off her—I thought she needed to stand on her own feet. I never imagined she'd mess up her life like this.'

'Maybe we're worrying for nothing,' said Talia, more to console herself than him. 'They might not even be together, or if they are they might just be having a bit of a holiday. Nothing serious.' But even as she spoke the words she did not really believe them.

They went back to the office and Dervan rang around several of Emilio's friends, but no one knew where he had gone. In fact they did not even know that he had gone away. But they promised to get in touch if they heard anything.

'There's not much we can do now except wait until we hear from your sister,' said Dervan gravely.

Talia nodded.

'I'll get Maria to make you some coffee.'

'Thank you.' She sat on the edge of her seat in his office, her fingers twisting in her lap, her face serious, trying to decide what to do next. She could wait for days, weeks even. In fact Serine might not even bother to get in touch with Dervan. Her sister could be pretty casual about things like that.

Her coffee came and she sipped it, while Dervan went through some papers on his desk. But finally he put down his pen and looked at her. 'I think, Talia, that you ought to keep yourself occupied. How do you feel about assisting Maria again? The computer's arriving in a few days. I could do with your help.'

Her eyes were dull as she lifted her head. 'I suppose I could. I don't fancy going back to England until I've heard something. On the other hand, she might try to get in touch with me there. Oh, Dervan, what if she does, and I'm not at home? What if she needs me?'

'Your best bet,' he said firmly, 'is to wait

here. Emilio won't be away long. He likes to keep an eagle eye on his shops.'

'Are you sure?' A faint light of hope shone in her eyes.

'As sure as I can be in the circumstances.'

'Then,' she said slowly, 'I think I'll start work now. I need something to keep my mind off Serine.' Though somehow she doubted whether she would be able to concentrate.

Maria was more than pleased to help, and she expressed her sympathy over Talia's missing sister. 'I do not know where she is—she say nothing. I thought maybe she go back to England. She was not happy after Paul left.'

Talia frowned. 'Not happy? But I thought she had a new boyfriend—Emilio something or other.'

The dark girl nodded. 'Yes. She speak of him plenty, but she not in love.' Maria lifted her shoulders expansively. 'She use him, I think. He has a lot of money—more than Senor Deville.'

'Did she ever say anything to you about going away with Emilio?'

Maria thought for a moment. 'No, I do not think so. But yes—wait a minute, she say that Emilio, he have to go to Gran Canaria, to Las Palmas. Somebody sick—an uncle, I think. Serine go with him, you think?'

'She may have done.' Talia's face lit up. 'Oh, Maria, thank you. *Thank you.*' She hurried out of the office and back in to Dervan, telling him what his secretary had said. 'Can we go?' she asked. 'I'm sure Serine must be there.'

'Have you any idea of the population of Las Palmas?' he asked, with an indulgent smile. 'About three hundred and fifty thousand. How are we going to find them?'

'But his office, his home—somebody, surely, they'll have an address?' Her initial enthusiasm began to fade.

'Not necessarily,' he said, 'but if that is where they've gone then I don't think we need worry too much. They'll be back shortly.'

'I hope you're right,' said Talia, her shoulders drooping.

Dervan got up from his desk and came across to her, lifting her chin with a gentle finger. 'Look on the bright side! If he has a sick uncle to look after he won't be spending much time with your sister. In fact I can't understand why she went with him.'

'Nor can I,' she confessed, and wished he would move. Even in the midst of her anguish Talia was still sufficiently aware of him to be disturbed by his nearness.

The rest of the day dragged, and when Dervan took her back to his villa Talia went to her room and lay down. She was there so long that he came looking for her.

'I thought you'd gone to sleep,' he said.

Talia was so dispirited that she could not even tell him off for entering her room without knocking. She sat up, hunching her knees under her chin and wrapping her arms around her legs. 'I was thinking,' she told him.

'It won't bring her back any sooner,' he said. 'I suggest you get dressed up and we'll go out for a meal.'

'I'd rather eat here,' she replied. 'I want to be here in case the phone goes, in case Serine tries to get in touch.'

After a shower and a change of clothes she felt better. Dervan cooked her an omelette and she did her best to eat it, but it was like swallowing sawdust.

Afterwards they sat outside enjoying the warm evening air, but neither of them spoke very much, and soon Talia declared she was going to bed.

Paul rang the office the next day, and was distraught when he heard the news. 'Is there nothing you can do? The police, perhaps? They would help track her down.'

'She's not exactly a missing person yet,' answered Talia softly. 'Dervan has every faith that they'll return in a few days.'

'A few days! To hell with my job, Talia, I'm flying out. I'll be there just as soon as I can.'

'Paul, that's not the answer. There's nothing you can do. I'll ring you the instant I hear anything.'

There was a long silence, then he said, 'You're right. But I'm still coming out there. Another week should see this job through and then I'll be on my way.'

Talia hoped that Serine would be back before then. But day followed day and they heard nothing, and she grew more and more worried. She hardly slept at night and Dervan did his best to console her. He was a perfect friend and companion, and she did not know what she would have done without him.

Her distress drew them closer together, and although he never made any sexual advances he often put his arm about her as they sat together after dinner. On one occasion she actually went to sleep in his arms and woke up in bed. She had her nightdress on, and went hot at the thought of Dervan undressing her. But he never mentioned it and neither did she.

They had got into the habit of having their evening meal in his villa, cooked by the local woman who also did some cleaning. Talia was afraid to go out in case she missed a call from Serine.

On Sunday evening, three days later, they were lingering at the table after their meal when they suddenly heard a desperate sobbing. Whirling in their chairs, they saw Serine standing in the doorway. Talia sprang to her feet, but Dervan was the one to reach her sister before she collapsed.

CHAPTER NINE

Dervan lifted Serine and carried her across to the settee, where he laid her gently down. Talia was aghast at her sister's appearance. Normally Serine was immaculate, now she looked as though she had been sleeping in her clothes. Her hair hadn't been washed or combed for days, she wore no make-up and was deathly pale, with huge purple shadows beneath her eyes.

Kneeling down, Talia took Serine's hand in hers, tears streaming down her face. 'Serine, what's happened? Oh, Serine, tell me! I've been worried out of my mind!'

The younger girl's eyes focused on Talia. 'What—' she asked faintly, 'are you doing here?'

'Never mind that now,' said Talia. 'I want to know what's happened to you.'

'Is Emilio the cause of this?' asked Dervan, a hardness in his voice that Talia had not heard in days.

'Emilio?' A scared expression came into Serine's eyes.

'Yes, Emilio,' he said strongly. 'Where is he?'

'I—he—I don't know. I ran away. He was—oh, God!' She shuddered and put her hands over her face, starting to cry again.

'Leave her,' said Talia softly, and to Serine, 'Come on, I'll get you cleaned up and into bed. You'll feel better once you've had some sleep.'

But Serine no longer had the strength to walk. His face tight with suppressed anger, Dervan swung her up into his arms and carried her through into the bedroom next to Talia's.

Talia motioned for him to leave, but he stood there resolutely while she stripped off Serine's clothes, and then she could see why he had insisted on staying. The bruises on Serine's body were horrifying.

Talia gasped, even Dervan looked shocked. 'I'm going to find that bastard,' he whipped, 'and kill him!' He swung out of the room, and Talia was too concerned with Serine to stop him.

She gently sponged her sister, and brushed her hair, then slid one of her own nighties over Serine's head and helped her into bed. 'I'll heat you some milk,' she said. 'You'll feel better with something hot inside you, and afterwards you can sleep for as long as you like.'

She contemplated fetching a doctor, but Serine was too exhausted at this stage to suffer an examination and questioning. There would be time for that later. In fact Serine was already asleep when Talia returned with the milk. She put it down and drew up a chair to the side of the bed, keeping a vigil over her sister right through the night. Dervan never returned.

The next morning he phoned to ask how Serine was and to say that he was in Las

Palmas. He hadn't found Emilio yet, but he had an address.

'You won't do anything stupid?' asked Talia anxiously.

'I'll do what I have to do,' he snarled, and put down the phone.

Serine did not wake until almost lunchtime, but when she did she felt strong enough to take a shower and wash her hair. After that she ate a little of the chicken salad Talia had prepared and drank several cups of coffee.

It was not until they went outside to sit in the garden that Talia questioned her sister, even though it had been hard to hold her tongue.

'I thought Emilio really loved me,' Serine admitted. 'I didn't love him, but I didn't think that mattered. He could give me the lifestyle I craved. But all he wanted was—my body.' Her voice broke as she made her confession.

Talia closed her eyes at the thought of this brute mauling her sister.

'He said we were going to stay with his uncle, but it was a lie. He took me to this house, and there was only the two of us. He—he was like an animal. I'd always refused to let him make love to me—I said he'd got to wait until we were married. He never meant to marry me, Talia, he just wanted his evil way.'

'So what happened?' asked Talia, her eyes filling with tears. She hoped with all her heart this man hadn't actually raped her sister.

'We were fighting in the kitchen—I threw pepper in his face—and then ran away. Oh, Talia, it was awful! I never expected, I never—'

'Shh!' Talia took her sister's trembling body into her arms, feeling a stone-cold hatred for Emilio. What type of a man was he, that he could treat an eighteen-year-old like this? 'It's all over now, but I really think we ought to call the police,' she said.

'No! Please, no!' cried Serine at once.

'He's too powerful a man. He'd say I'd led him on, and actually I did go away with him, so I have only myself to blame. I just never knew he was like that.'

'I suppose you're right,' Talia agreed, 'but Serine, how could you have gone out with him in the first place? According to Dervan he was far too old for you.'

'I didn't think age mattered,' whimpered Serine.

'It was his money that interested you?'

Serine nodded. 'But I'm beginning to realise that money isn't everything. Some of the best men are the ones without it.'

'Such as Paul?' asked Talia quietly.

Serine nodded. 'I feel awful about him. He loved me, you know, and I let him down. I think I was actually half-way to falling in love with him, except that I had this obsession about wanting to marry a rich man.'

'And now?' asked Talia quietly.

'Now I don't want any man, not for a long time. But when I do I'll look for someone nearer my own age, someone like Paul. I sometimes wish I'd never let him go.'

Talia decided to let Paul's arrival be a surprise for Serine. If her sister knew he was coming she might refuse to see him. Talia had already phoned Paul early that morning and told him about Serine's condition, and he was booking himself on the first available flight.

She kept wishing Dervan would return. He had been angry enough to carry out his threat to kill Emilio. What if he had? What if even at this moment the police were hunting him? He might even be in prison! Tears filled her eyes at the thought, and for the rest of the day her mind was in turmoil.

After her sister had gone to bed Talia sat on the settee where she and Dervan had spent most of their evenings while waiting for news of Serine. She felt close to him here, and she could even detect the faint lingering odour of his aftershave. The minutes ticked by like hours and the hours like days, and she wished she knew what had happened, where he was, whether he would be coming home soon.

She closed her eyes and must have slept, because the next thing she knew Dervan was touching her shoulder. He looked desperately tired, he needed a shave, and one eye was swollen and bruised. But he was safe and he was in one piece, and Talia jumped to her feet 'Dervan—oh, *Dervan!* Thank God you're home safe! I've been so worried about you.' Instinctively she put her arms around him, holding him close, relief flooding into her.

'If this is the sort of reception I get, perhaps I should go away more often,' he smiled, returning her embrace, holding her so tightly he was in danger of squeezing all the breath out of her.

She turned her face up to his, her love shining in her eyes, and he bent his head and kissed her.

Talia poured every amount of feeling

she possessed into that kiss, giving herself away, but not caring. He was back, he was safe, and oh, how she loved him!

Then just as suddenly he let her go. 'I'm sorry, I shouldn't have done that.' The mask of indifference began to fall over his face again.

'Yes, Dervan, *yes!*' she protested firmly. 'I want you to kiss me, and hold me. I never want you to let me go. Dervan, I love you, and I want to marry you—if you still want me?'

He looked as though he couldn't believe what he had heard. His eyes narrowed and he held her at arm's length, looking at her carefully. 'Talia, you do know what you're saying?'

'I know, and I don't care if you don't love me, I love you enough for the two of us. You've no idea how worried I've been about you. I've been absolutely sick with fear!'

He did not kiss her again as she had thought he would. He continued to look at her, and Talia grew restless with impatience. 'Aren't you going to say anything? Am I making a fool of myself? Have you changed your mind?' A chill struck through her at the thought.

'Talia, of course not.' He at last held her to him. 'I came back so tired and despondent, worried about Serine, angry with Emilio, then I find you waiting up for me, and this. It's more than I ever expected. Thank you, Talia. You'll never regret it, I promise you.'

They clung together for several more minutes, then Talia withdrew and insisted on bathing his eye. 'Serine's much better,' she said, as she held a cold compress over his wound.

'Yes, I looked in on her before I woke you. Did she tell you what happened?'

Talia nodded.

'She was lucky to get away from him. I always knew he had a penchant for young women, but I've since discovered that this isn't the first time he's tried to take them by force. I think I should go to the police.'

Talia shook her head. 'Serine's made me promise not to. She said he'd be sure to win because she went with him voluntarily.'

'That could very well be the case,' he agreed, 'but there's one consolation, he won't be in a fit state to force himself on another girl for a long, long time, if ever. You might think my eye looks bad, but you should see Emilio!'

Talia shuddered. 'I hate violence.'

Instantly Dervan gathered her to him, one hand soothingly stroking her hair. 'It was necessary,' he said, 'but if this whole affair has taught Serine a lesson, then maybe we shouldn't feel so bad about it.'

Talia nodded. 'I think she has learned her lesson. I phoned Paul. He was horrified, and he's coming as soon as he can. I have a feeling things might begin to work out for them after all.'

'I suggest we now forget the whole episode,' said Dervan. 'I'm starving. What have we got to eat?'

'There are eggs in the fridge, I could make you an omelette,' she offered.

'Wonderful! I'll take a shower while you do it.'

When Dervan returned wearing nothing but a short towelling robe she felt the excitement mount in her. They sat at the kitchen table, Talia watching him while he ate, unable to take her eyes off him. This was the man she was going to marry, this man with the black eye and the tanned muscular chest. This was the first of many times that she would sit opposite him at the table. It felt good, really good.

'Do you know, Talia,' he said, pausing as he forked fluffy omelette into his mouth, 'tonight is the first time you've actually told me that you love me. I knew you felt a physical attraction, but when you kept refusing to marry me I couldn't be sure whether it was anything more.'

'I think I've always loved you,' she said quietly.

His mouth twisted wryly. 'I feel a heel. It's not fair to let you marry me on those terms. If neither of us was in love we could afford to take the risk but with you feeling as you do I might end up breaking your heart.'

'That is my risk,' she said. 'It's my gamble. *I* asked *you* this time. I'm quite sure it will work out, but if it doesn't you must never blame yourself.'

Dervan put down his knife and fork and took her hands across the table. 'Talia, I don't deserve a girl like you.'

'Please don't say that. Please don't spoil things for me,' she said, her voice pained. 'Who knows, perhaps one day you might—' The words would not come.

'If it's within my power, Talia, then I will. If there's a person I could fall in love with, it's you. But I can't help what's happened in here.' He thumped his heart with his fist. 'All I can say is, if you want to go through with this marriage, then I'll try my damnedest never to let you regret it.'

There was so much emotion in his eyes that Talia felt sure he must love her, even though he could not find it in him to admit it. 'I want to marry you,' she said, her own voice choked with a similar emotion.

He nodded, only the slightest movement of his head, his mouth clamped shut, his eyes coal-black and nerve-tinglingly sensual.

His omelette was forgotten as he pushed his chair back from the table and stood up. Talia rose too, and their bodies came together like a meeting of souls. This was a moment to surpass all moments, a commitment a promise. She had never been so happy in her life.

It was early morning before they went to bed. They had so much to talk about, so much to discuss. Talia refused to dwell on the fact that Dervan did not love her.

It seemed of little consequence. Even if he was afraid to fall in love he was still sufficiently fond of her to want to make her happy. And with that, for the moment anyway, she was content.

Despite going to bed late and having no sleep the night before Talia was up early. She wanted to tell Serine about the wedding, though she was a little dubious as to what sort of reception the news would get. She couldn't be quite certain that Serine had got over Dervan.

Her sister was wide awake, sitting up in bed, thumbing through a magazine. 'I heard you and Dervan talking last night,' she said at once. 'Did he find Emilio?'

'Yes, he found him,' said Talia gently, 'and from all accounts they had quite a punch-up.'

'Who won?'

'Dervan, of course.'

'What did Emilio say? Did he try to find me?'

Talia shook her head. 'I've no idea. If I were you, Serine, I'd push the whole episode right out of your life.'

'It will take a long time to do that,' said Serine, 'but I'm determined never to be so stupid again.'

'I guess you learned your lesson the hard way?'

Serine nodded. 'Thank you for not saying "I told you so".'

'You're my sister, and I love you,' said Talia, hugging her. 'But now I have some good news.' She could keep it to herself no longer. 'Dervan and I are going to get married.' She held her breath, waiting for Serine's response, mentally crossing her fingers that her sister wouldn't bear any resentment.

But after her initial surprise, Serine smiled happily. 'I'm pleased for you, Talia. You deserve someone like Dervan. He's a man in a million—I realise that now.'

'He is,' agreed Talia.

'He never tried to take advantage of me,

even though I virtually threw myself at him. He's not like Emilio,' Serine added bitterly.

Talia hugged her sister yet again, and at that moment Dervan walked in through the open door. 'It's good to see that at last you're behaving how sisters should,' he remarked.

'And we will for ever more,' confirmed Serine stoutly. 'I owe you an apology too, Dervan. I'm sorry for the way I've behaved.'

'I tried to teach you a lesson myself,' he confessed, 'by going out with other girls and showing you that you can't possess a man through sheer persistence. I wish it had worked. It would have saved you going through this hell.'

Serine shuddered. 'I'll never forget what Emilio did to me, and I'm truly grateful to you for going after him. Talia says you gave him a beating, but it doesn't look as though you got off scot-free yourself.' She looked at his black eye ruefully. 'I'm sorry—I seem to have caused a lot of trouble all round.'

'Talia says you don't want to press charges?'

'Most definitely not. I just want to push the whole thing out of my mind.' She paused a moment reflectively, then said with a bright smile, 'I believe congratulations are in order?'

Dervan glanced at Talia. 'You've told her?'

Talia nodded happily. 'I had to tell someone,' and then to Serine, 'Will you be my bridesmaid?'

Serine nodded. 'Try stopping me! When is the great day to be?'

'As soon as it can be arranged,' replied Talia, glancing shyly at Dervan as she spoke.

'And where? Here?'

'No.' This time Dervan spoke. 'In England, of course, but we're going to live here until I've finished this project. After that we're going to buy a house and settle in England. We want a family, and I happen to think that they should have stable roots.'

'I wish it were me,' said Serine with faint regret.

Talia thought of Paul and smiled. 'Your turn will come.'

Throughout the day Talia and Dervan did their best to entertain Serine, but there were moments when she withdrew deep within herself, and Talia knew it would take time for her to recover.

The next day Dervan went to work and just after lunch Paul arrived. Serine was lying out in the garden and Talia answered the door. His normally cheerful face was creased with worry and his first words were, 'How is Serine?'

'Improving,' said Talia cheerfully, while motioning him inside.

'Did you tell her I was coming?'

'No,' she admitted. 'Actually, she's a bit off men at the moment.'

'Understandable,' he said. 'I'll be very

gentle. Where is she?'

'Outside. I'll tell her you're here.'

'No.' He put up a hand to stop her. 'Let me surprise her.'

A few minutes later Serine and Paul came into the house with their arms around one another, and Talia knew everything was going to be all right.

In Paul's company Serine improved rapidly and in a few days was ready to go back to work, Paul spent some time in the office too, making sure the new computer would do everything Dervan wanted, and teaching Maria how to use it as well.

Talia arranged to go home to organise the wedding and sort out her own business. The house was going to be transferred to Serine, and Talia hoped that one day she and Paul might get married and live there. It was far too soon at the moment though, to talk about such a possibility.

'I wish I could come with you,' said Dervan. 'But things are moving rapidly here and need constant supervision.'

Talia wished he could too. She was going to miss him. They had become so close during the last few days that it would be like splitting herself in two.

On the Saturday evening before her flight Dervan suggested they all go to Jameos del Agua. It was, by day, an alluring tropical grotto, by night a spectacular nightclub. Talia had heard mention of it many times and she clapped her hands with joy. 'Yes, please, I'd like that.'

In his car on the way Dervan told them a little bit about the place. 'It's actually a tunnel left by a lava flow and turned into an incredible grotto. César Manrique is responsible for it. He's a well-known artist but also unofficial cultural mandarin of the island. He did the landscaping at Fire Mountain as well as various other projects. He always works hand in glove with nature. He's a genius.'

There was no hint on the surface of the beauty that was to meet their eyes. They went into what appeared to be a low stone building, paid their money, then descended an iron spiral staircase into the caves themselves.

Both Talia and Serine gasped when they saw it. It was like fairyland. The whole cave had been thoughtfully and carefully landscaped. There were cactus plants thirty feet tall, ferns in huge hanging baskets, hibiscus in full flower, palm trees, more cacti. Lights were hidden in strategic places and faint but audible music set the mood.

Talia caught Dervan's hand. 'This is absolutely fantastic! I've never seen anything like it.' Her eyes shone with happiness and wonderment as she looked from one incredible thing to another. She wore a pale blue dress with a full skirt and a square low neck, and her chestnut hair fell in deep waves about her shoulders.

Dervan smiled indulgently and bending his head low kissed her. 'You look like Alice in Wonderland.'

'I feel like her. It's out of this world!'

The cave in which they stood had been converted into a restaurant. There were black iron tables, and chairs with orange padded seats, and above, where the cave was open to the night sky, an orange cover had been drawn, to give some protection from the cool evening air.

The floor was uneven, and Talia clung to Dervan as she looked around. There was a dance floor and one side of the area overlooked a lake. 'There are tiny blind white crabs in there,' he told her, 'that are supposedly found nowhere else in the world. And the lake's actually tidal, in contact with the sea through small underground galleries.'

Talia found it the most fascinating experience of her life. They had already lost Serine and Paul, but she did not mind. She preferred to be alone with Dervan.

'We'll eat first then go and explore later,' he said.

Dining in what had once been a tunnel full of molten lava was a unique experience, and Talia could not stop looking around her. Dervan was continually amused by her excitement. 'I should have brought you here sooner,' he said.

'You should. I can't get over it—it's absolutely fantastic!' Her whole face was alight with enthusiasm.

He reached across the table and taking her hand lifted it to his mouth. 'You're the one who's fantastic. You're the one who's turning this into a magical experience. I love watching you.'

They finished their meal and hand in hand walked along the narrow path that ran beside the lake. Talia was thrilled when she saw the minute albinic crabs.

Beyond the lake was yet another dance floor and a bar, and they sat there for while, sipping drinks and letting the atmosphere of the place build up around them.

When they finally moved further along the tunnel Talia was enthralled to discover a swimming pool surrounded by gardens filled with palms and exotic plants. Here it was open to the sky, and it really was a wonderland.

Talia thought that this was all there was to see, and was amazed when Dervan led her through a door into yet another cave that had been converted into an auditorium. There were rows and rows of black seats tiered down to the stage.

'They hold orchestral concerts here,' explained Dervan. 'Also ballet and opera. The acoustics are brilliant.'

At the back of the stage ran a waterfall, and behind it was another room with a transparent domed roof. A glass mobile hung and glittered from its centre like a giant Christmas tree decoration.

They walked back to the rows of seats and sat down. Mood music played very softly in the background and the atmosphere was indescribable. It was full of emotion. It soothed and relaxed and made Talia want to sit there for ever.

When they finally walked back to the dance floor they were both silent, and when Dervan took her into his arms and they moved slowly to the music she wanted the moment to go on for ever. She felt more close to Dervan here than she had ever done before.

But then suddenly the floor was cleared for a display of Lanzarote folk dancing and the mood was quickly dispelled as lively music filled the air. The men were dressed in blue, the women in long colourful dresses with aprons over them, and all wearing traditional straw hats.

It was a lively scene, and most enjoyable, but Talia preferred the poetic atmosphere of the mood music. 'Let's go back into the auditorium,' she whispered when the dancers had finished.

They found Serine and Paul in there. sitting quietly, absolute peace on their faces. Talia could not remember ever having seen Serine so tranquil. This place really did have a magical effect.

Joining them on the same row of seats, they spent well over thirty minutes just sitting there soaking up the atmosphere. Dervan held Talia's hand and looked at her constantly, and it was as though they were alone in the whole universe.

It grew late, and he suggested a last dance before they left. Talia's love for him had never been so intense, and she melted in his arms and hid none of her feelings. She was not afraid now to show him how much she loved him. And when she looked into his face she was sure there was love in his eyes too. Or was it purely desire? Was that still all he felt for her? A shadow crossed her face at the thought. Dervan saw it and frowned. 'Is something wrong?' he queried.

Talia shook her head, but the suspicion was still there, and some of her happiness evaporated.

'You look worried all of a sudden.'

'It's nothing,' she insisted.

'I don't believe you.'

Talia shrugged, unable to tell him what she was thinking. He had never attempted to make any secret of the way he felt and she had accepted him as he was. There was no point in getting cold feet now.

On the drive home Dervan was broodingly silent, and he failed to kiss her goodnight when they went to their respective rooms. Talia felt close to tears, and again it was all her own fault She should have kept her feelings hidden.

She slept little and got up early to finish her packing. They all breakfasted together, but Serine and Paul had eyes only for each other, noticing nothing wrong between Talia and Dervan.

It was not until they were on their way to the airport that he said, 'If you want to change your mind about marrying me, Talia, then don't be afraid to say so.'

Talia started to cry. 'Of course I don't want to change my mind. I love you.' And then as the thought struck her, 'How about you, Dervan, do you want to back out?'

He gave an impatient toss of his head. 'What a ridiculous question!'

'But you're cross with me.'

'Disappointed, not cross, Talia. I detected a change in you last night, and I want to know why you won't tell me what's wrong.'

Because you'll say that I'm having second thoughts and the wedding should be called off, and I don't want that. I want to marry you more than anything else in the whole wide world. 'There's nothing wrong,' she insisted. 'You jumped to the wrong conclusion because I had an unhappy thought. Doesn't everyone at some time?'

'Not in last night's circumstances. I thought the whole setting was perfect.'

'It was,' she protested. 'Please, Dervan, don't let's fall out over nothing. I want to go back to England with happy thoughts in my mind. How can I arrange the wedding if I don't even know whether you're friends with me?'

When he stopped the car at the airport he turned in his seat and pulled her to him. 'Talia, my feelings haven't changed one iota. It's yours I'm worried about.'

'I love you,' she said firmly. 'And I pray that one day you'll be able to love me. Until then I'm content to settle for whatever you offer.'

He looked deep into her eyes. 'No doubts at all?'

'None.' Her eyes did not waver as she looked at him, and with a groan he tightened his arms round her and his mouth came down on hers. The kiss said everything. Talia held nothing back and neither, it seemed, did he.

They were both shaken when they finally pulled apart, and it was a few minutes before they had the strength to get out of the car and walk through into the departure lounge.

Talia did not want to go now, she wanted to wait until Dervan could come with her. But someone had to make the arrangements. Besides, a few weeks, that was all it would be, and then they would be together forever. Forever! How good that sounded.

The house felt empty when Talia finally arrived back in England, but she had lots to do, and the time passed quickly.

Dervan phoned her the next day, and the line was so clear it was as though he was in the same town.

'I'm missing you already,' she complained.

'Me too, Talia. Have you fixed anything up yet?'

She grinned into the phone. 'I went to see the vicar. He thought it most odd that I was doing all the arranging alone. And he insists that you go to see him before the wedding.'

'I think you've forgotten a slight detail,' Dervan said. 'Isn't the date more important than how the vicar reacted?'

'Oh, Dervan, I'm sorry,' Talia giggled into the phone. 'It's the thirtieth—four weeks on Saturday. I wish it weren't so long, but the banns have to be read.'

'Dammit, Talia,' he said in a sudden loud voice, 'you shouldn't be doing this. I'm coming over.'

'But your work?'

'They'll have to get along without me,' he growled, 'and if anything goes wrong then it will have to be put right when I get back. Expect me some time tomorrow.'

'Yes, Dervan,' she said, but the phone had already gone dead.

Talia felt thrilled at the thought of seeing him again when she had expected a whole month to pass. She spent the rest of the day polishing and cleaning, shopping and baking.

Early the next morning she showered and washed her hair, and was on tenterhooks waiting for Dervan to arrive.

In the event it was late afternoon before a car finally pulled up outside her house. She ran outside to meet him, feeling as though they had been apart for weeks instead of a couple of days.

Dervan swung her up in his arms and whirled her around. 'Sorry it took so long getting here, but I had something to organise.' He set her down and pulled a sheet of folded paper out of his pocket. 'A special licence. We're getting married at the weekend. I decided I couldn't wait for a whole month!'

CHAPTER TEN

A special licence! Did this mean, thought Talia, that Dervan was at last admitting he loved her? But he did not say so. He took her hand and they walked into the house, and once the door was closed he kissed her soundly. Talia felt her whole body pulse into life and she pressed herself against him, feeling his instantaneous response.

'I hope you don't mind my changing your plans?' he asked, when he finally managed to drag himself away.

'Mind? I'm delighted,' she replied, her eyes shining with excitement. 'I couldn't bear the thought either of waiting a whole month. But you haven't given me much time to choose my dress.'

'Your outfit is in my car,' he smiled. 'Again I took the liberty.'

Talia shook her head. 'I've never met a man like you, Dervan Deville!'

'Which is fortunate for me,' he grinned. 'Otherwise you'd have fallen in love with him. Have you got anything to eat? I'm starving!'

'I've a casserole in the oven,' Talia told him. It had seemed the best thing to prepare when she did not know what time he was arriving.

After their meal they sat and talked and finalised their plans. They held hands and kissed, and Talia felt everything a bride should. The lack of three little words made not an atom of difference.

Dervan fetched her dress from the car, but he would not let her look at it in his presence. 'When I've gone,' he kept repeating.

'But what if it doesn't fit?'

'It will.'

'How do you know?'

'Because, my lovely Talia, I know more about you than you know yourself.'

He left at about half-past ten, and the first thing Talia did was open the box that contained her wedding dress. She gasped aloud as she lifted it out. It was ivory satin embroidered with seed pearls and mother-of-pearl sequins. It fastened very demurely right to the throat with long leg-of-mutton sleeves and a full skirt with more pearls and sequins around the hem. It was a fairy-tale dress, and when she tried it on, true to Dervan's prediction, it fitted perfectly.

As Talia lay in bed that night it suddenly came to her why Dervan had changed the arrangements, and she wondered why she had not thought of it before. His fiancée, all those years ago, had died a week before the wedding. The second girl he loved had walked out on him when they began making arrangements. He was afraid something might happen to stop him getting married this third time, but it wouldn't. She was very, very sure of her feelings for him. He was worrying for nothing.

The next couple of days fled. Serine and Paul arrived, Serine bringing her dress with her also, a deep jade green satin that perfectly complemented her auburn hair.

Dervan had invited Paul to be his best man, and Talia asked their next-door neighbour, a man who had been a very good friend of her father, to give her away. Both he and his wife were surprised to hear she was getting married at such short notice, and Talia could imagine a certain amount of tongue-wagging and speculation behind her back. But they were a nice couple for all that and he said he would be delighted to take her father's place.

Talia went through the wedding ceremony with her head in the clouds. It was as though it was happening to someone else. All she remembered was the vicar saying, 'I now pronounce you man and wife.'

At those words she looked at Dervan, so tall and magnificent in his grey morning suit and all the love she felt for him welled up in her eyes.

'You may kiss the bride,' said the vicar.

Dervan needed no second bidding, but the kiss was of necessity disappointingly brief.

After the photographs had been taken and a short reception held in a local hotel, Dervan whisked her away in his car for their two-day honeymoon in a London hotel. 'I'm sorry it's not anywhere more exotic,' he had said when he told her of the arrangement, 'but as we're going to spend the whole of the time in bed I don't suppose it really matters.'

Talia had gone like jelly at the thought and now that they were alone his words came back. As if guessing what was in her mind, Dervan reached across and took her hand. 'Well, Mrs Deville, how do you feel now it's all over?'

But it wasn't over, was it? They were united in name, but not yet in body. That was when she would consider herself well and truly married. Even so she had a sense of belonging, and her whole body was vibrantly alive. 'As if I'm floating on a cloud,' she answered.

His eyes twinkled. 'Don't float too far away, because I intend, as soon as is decently possible, to make you mine in every sense of the word.' His hand tightened on hers as he spoke, and Talia's eyes shone with love as she looked at him.

It was early evening when they arrived, and Dervan had arranged to have dinner sent to their room. Privately Talia did not think she would be able to eat; her excitement was too great.

The bridal suite had a pastel blue carpet and blue, rose and cream furnishings. The bed was huge with a cleverly draped canopy and there were two settees, a writing desk, a television, mirrors hidden in the wall panelling, and a bathroom as large as Talia's sitting-room at home.

'It's like something out of a film set!' she gasped.

He smiled at her enthusiasm, and took

her into his arms. 'Talia, my beautiful Talia, this is the moment I've been waiting for.'

Unbidden came the thought that he was lusting after her body, but she squashed it at once as unworthy. They had gone over that once. And in all honesty her body was as eager to be possessed as his was to possess her.

Dervan traced the outline of her face with gentle fingers, kissing her, looking at her, holding her. Talia's desire began to mount. And then came a cautious tap on the door. Their dinner had arrived!

She expected Dervan to express irritation at being disturbed. It was, after all, their first real moment alone as man and wife. But he merely smiled and kissed the tip of her nose. 'More later,' he promised.

Beneath silver-covered dishes on the trolley they found *souchet* of sole, Charentais melon with grapes, pheasant *en cocotte* with *château* potatoes and braised celery, and a delicious raspberry soufflé for dessert, decorated with crystallised violets and rose petals. It was a feast fit for a king, and although Talia had doubted her ability to eat she soon discovered that she was starving.

Dervan rarely took his eyes off her. They made love to her, lingering on the thrust of her breasts through the grey silk of her blouse. Her nipples hardened in anticipation. He watched her mouth as she ate and more than once he reached out across the table and touched her lips. 'You're beautiful, Talia,' he whispered.

They toasted each other in champagne, and Talia made a silent wish that Dervan would one day find the courage to admit that he loved her. She felt sure that he could not be acting and speaking in this way if he didn't. He was so gentle, so considerate, so kind, so patient. He was everything she had ever wanted in a man and thought she would never find. Her years of denial while looking after Serine had made her give up hope.

When they finished their meal and the trolley was wheeled away by a white-coated waiter, Talia unpacked and hung away their clothes, putting their toothbrushes in the bathroom, side by side. It gave her a nice feeling, this togetherness. Dervan watched every move that she made—he seemed to find pleasure in watching her—and when she had finished he held out his arms and she went willingly into them.

He was in no hurry to make love to her. Talia had always had visions of newlyweds being unable to wait, of stripping off their clothes the second they were alone and making instant and violent love. Dervan wasn't like that. He kissed her first of all, her eyes, her nose, her ears, the corners of her mouth, inside her lower lip—every movement calculated and sensual, driving her crazy with desire.

And then, and only then, he very slowly began to undress her, touching and kissing every inch of skin as it was exposed—her breasts, her stomach, her hips, her thighs.

It was a long-drawn-out process, and by the time she was completely naked Talia felt as though her whole body was on fire. Her pulses were racing, her heart thumping, and the excitement was unbearable.

Dervan stepped back a pace and looked at her, and Talia surprised herself by not feeling shy.

I think,' she said, with a faint smile, 'that it's now my turn to undress you.'

It took a long time, because he kept kissing her and stroking her, but then he was finally naked, and suddenly his kisses were no longer tender or provocative, but deep and meaningful.

Without warning he lifted her in his arms and carried her to the bed, where his hands and his mouth explored every intimate part of her. Her whole body throbbed and pulsed and she clung to him, kissing him too, tasting him, feeling, half sobbing with the intensity of her passion.

She wanted him to make love to her, she wondered how much longer he was going to draw it out. How could he bear to wait? His arousal was complete, it had been for a long time, but still he tortured her body until in the end she could wait no longer. 'Dervan, please, please make love to me. *Now!* Oh, God, I can't wait any longer!' Her fingers bit into his shoulders and she strained her body against him.

With unbearable slowness he entered her, and apart from a brief moment of pain Talia reached a height of ecstasy never before imaginable. It ended all too quickly, a surge of sudden heat, a feeling that her body was going to explode, Dervan calling out as he reached his point of no return. A few convulsive movements, then their bodies relaxed. 'That's why I waited, Talia,' he said at length. 'I knew it would be over far too quickly. But next time I promise you it will be better.'

And it was, and the time after that, and again and again. During the next two days they were rarely out of each other's arms. Their meals arrived, and he fed her and she fed him. They did everything together. Talia didn't want the honeymoon to end. It was a time of sensuality and sexuality, of pagan lust and sensitive lovemaking. It was all and more than she could ever have wished for.

But it had to end, and on the morning of their departure Talia had tears in her eyes. 'Don't cry,' said Dervan, understanding her feelings, cupping her face and gently stroking away the tears with his thumbs. 'This is the beginning, not the end.'

'It's been so beautiful here,' she whispered.

'And it will be in Lanzarote, I promise you.'

'Really?' she asked.

'Really. I'll do my best to make every day special.'

In the chartered plane he treated her as though she were a piece of Dresden china. Did she want this, or that? Was she comfortable, hungry, thirsty? He made love to her with exquisite tenderness one moment and animal hunger the next. He looked at her with love in his eyes, but never once did he say that he loved her. This was Talia's only disappointment.

Maybe it wouldn't have meant much to some people, but to her it meant everything. She wanted to be loved, she needed it. Ever since her parents' accident she had had no one to love her, not really love her. Serine had always taken her so much for granted. And she had dreamt of the day she would find herself a husband who would tell her this morning, noon and night.

She forced herself not to think of it, and as the days and weeks passed her contentment grew. Serine returned and finished her designs for Dervan, then went back home to England—to Paul. She was a different girl altogether, and Talia was very happy for her.

Talia helped out in the office, and Dervan spent a lot of time overseeing the building—not that he had to, but it was his baby and he wanted to watch its development every step of the way. The villas were growing at an impressive rate now that all the foundations had been laid, and Talia could see better what Dervan was striving to achieve. 'I wouldn't mind living in one myself,' she said to him one day. 'Views of the sea, constant sunshine, luxury appointments—what else could you ask for?'

'That can be arranged,' was his instant response. 'It can be our holiday home.'

There was nothing she asked for that she did not get, and Talia learned not to always voice her thoughts or desires, because his generosity was embarrassing.

She had thought that life might settle into a routine, but instead no two days were alike. Sometimes Dervan made love to her before going to the office; he seemed not to mind what time he went in. On other occasions he would be gone before she was even awake. When he did this he always left her a gift on the pillow—a Bird of Paradise flower, a hand-embroidered handkerchief, an antique silver coin. Nothing of any great value, but Talia treasured them all the same.

Sometimes, if she didn't go into the office too, he would come home unexpectedly and they would make love. He could not seem to get enough of her, and in all honesty Talia felt the same way. She wondered how long this 'honeymoon feeling' would last. She hoped for ever.

And at the end of the day Dervan would either ask his local lady to cook their dinner—he never allowed Talia to cook, he said there would be time for that when they had their house in England—or they would eat out. She never knew until he arrived home what they were going to do, and trying to guess what he would suggest was part of the excitement.

They had moonlight picnics on deserted beaches, and they dined at Arrecife's most expensive hotels. They visited all the popular tourist spots, as well as seeking out little-known places.

Talia saw for herself the inlanders' unique way of growing vines. Each vine was planted in a hollow within a metre-high semi-circle of lava stones. The ground was then covered with black volcanic ash. It was an impressive sight along each side of the road and up the sides of the mountains. 'Why do they do it like that?' asked Talia.

'The walls protect the tender vines from the wind,' he told her, 'and the porous cinders soak up moisture out of the night air, feeding it to the plants, eliminating any need for rain. It's ingenious.'

'It's fantastic! I love this island, Dervan, it's so full of contrasts.'

Haria was another delightful village. 'The village of a thousand palms,' Dervan said, and she could see why. In contrast to the rest of this treeless island palms grew in profusion, little ones, big ones, medium-sized ones. 'Apparently,' he went on, 'it's tradition for each family to plant a palm tree every time a baby is born.'

'How do you know so much?' she frowned.

'Because I made it my duty to find out,' he told her. 'I visited almost every square inch of this island when I was looking for the right site for my villas.'

Life was idyllic, thought Talia. She had never in the whole of her twenty-eight years known such happiness. And when she discovered that she was pregnant her happiness increased tenfold.

She had at first thought that the emotional trauma of the wedding and her new life in Lanzarote had affected her normal bodily functions, and had said as much to Dervan, but as two months ran into three, she secretly paid a visit to the doctor. When she was given the good news she could not wait to tell Dervan. He would be ecstatic. He wanted children above all else.

The minute Dervan entered the house Talia's expression gave her away. 'Why are you looking like a cat who's stolen the cream?' he asked.

'Am I?'

'You know you are.'

Her arms went around him and she hugged him as tightly as she could. 'Dervan, guess what—I'm pregnant!'

'You're what?' His eyes widened in amazement. 'But you said that—'

'I know, I know,' she cut in. 'But it's true. I'm having your baby, Dervan.' And surely now he would tell her that he loved her?

But no. He kissed her and held her, gently, so gently, as though afraid of hurting the baby. He made her sit down and he brought her food and drink and he wouldn't let her do a thing. But not one word of love. It deepened the ache that lay buried in Talia's heart.

'I think you should go home to England,' he said one day a few weeks later when she was resting indoors after lunch. 'It's too hot for you here.'

'Only if you come too.'

'I can't, not yet' he said. 'This development is so important to me. But I'll come nearer the time—you know that I want to be there when my—when *our* son is born.'

His slip of the tongue made Talia recall their conversation when he had first asked her to marry him. He had wanted children before he got too old to enjoy them, he had said, and she had accused him of wanting a baby machine. He had insisted that wasn't true, but all of a sudden doubts beset her.

And it was there in her eyes, and he saw. But he misinterpreted the reason. 'Talia, don't distress yourself. All I want is what's best for you. I don't want to be parted, you should know that. I'll come home as often as I possibly can, I promise you.'

Talia turned her head away. 'I'm tired, Dervan, I want to go to sleep. Will you leave me alone for a while?'

Reluctantly he did so, but within minutes he was back. 'You're right Talia, I should come with you. It's unfair of me to expect you to go through all this alone. I'll make the arrangements.'

But the damage had been done. He was saying this now to please her, and Talia shook her head. 'It doesn't matter, Dervan. I understand how much everything means to you here. I'll go home alone, if that's what you want.'

'No!' He was definite about it now. 'Give me a few days to tie up the loose ends and we'll go together.'

Talia said nothing.

Dervan frowned. 'Is something else wrong, Talia? Are you not feeling well?'

'I'm all right,' she said.

He didn't believe her. He stood looking at her for several long moments, then he bent low and kissed her brow. 'Get some sleep,' he said softly, and left the room.

She heard him leave the villa and

immediately got up. How could she sleep? How could she even rest when her mind was in such turmoil? He had been so loving towards her during these past months that she had begun to think he really had married her for all the right reasons. It crucified her to discover that she was wrong.

As she paced up and down the room, as she sat down and then immediately stood up again, as she picked up a magazine, then threw it down, Talia wondered how she was going to cope. Could she put herself back on the same footing with Dervan knowing what she did?

She went outside and stood looking into the distance. It was cloudy—windy too, whipping her dress around her legs. Out to sea the sun silvered the water with dancing prisms of light. But the beauty of the scene held no fascination for her today. By one thoughtless word Dervan had brought her happiness crashing down about her head.

When he returned her mood had not

changed. He sat her on the settee beside him. 'Talia, if I upset you because I seemed eager to pack you off to England by yourself, then I apologise. I wasn't thinking. Hell, the last thing I want is to be parted from you. It's your health that concerns me, that's all. You seem to tire very easily in this heat.'

Talia allowed him to pull her into the crook of his arm, and he continued talking, and stroked her hair, and she wondered how a man who did not care could act in this manner. He was showing every sign of being a caring, loving husband and father-to-be. Perhaps she had over-reacted?

Gradually she relaxed, and as he continued to soothe her she managed to push her unkind thoughts to the back of her mind. They would never entirely go away, she knew that, but it was impossible to think ill of Dervan when he looked after her so ably, and especially when her body responded to his every second they were together.

'Better now?' he enquired at length.

Talia nodded.

He kissed her mouth tenderly, cupping her face, looking deep into her eyes. 'Talia, promise you'll always tell me if there's anything wrong. Don't bottle things up. I don't want to hurt you, ever. You mean too much to me.'

Me, or the baby? she almost said, but squashed the thought. He had no idea what he had said to upset her, and perhaps he hadn't meant it. Perhaps she had jumped to entirely the wrong conclusion. 'I promise,' she whispered.

Dervan smiled his satisfaction.

Several more days went by before he announced that he had booked their tickets and they were leaving at the end of the week.

'Both of us?' asked Talia.

'But of course.' His tone was mocking. 'Aren't you going to let me forget my one moment of self-indulgence?'

'Actually I feel guilty that you're leaving

your work on my account.'

'Talia! Don't ever feel that,' he ordered. 'I'm the one feeling guilty. But I've never before had a pregnant woman to look after.' He grinned benignly. 'I rather like it. I have a surprise for you as well, but you'll have to wait until we arrive in England to find out.'

'Oh, Dervan, tell me now,' she begged. 'You can't keep me in suspense for days and days. That's not fair!'

His lips quirked. 'Can't I? Just try me.' And no matter how many times she asked he wouldn't give her even the tiniest clue.

But when they arrived in England and he drove, not to her own house, nor to his London apartment but to a beautiful red brick Georgian house at Chiswick, she found out what it was.

'Dervan?' She looked at him with enquiring eyes as he drove straight up to the front door.

'My surprise,' he grinned.

'This is ours?'

'Yes.'

'But how? When? I can't believe it!' And if she had chosen it herself she couldn't be more delighted. It was absolutely perfect—roses rambling over the walls, velvet-smooth lawns, a walled garden that would be safe for the baby.

'Serine and Paul have been scouting around for me,' Dervan admitted. 'They've sent me photographs of dozens of places, but this was the one I thought you'd like best.'

'And I do, I do! Let's go inside—I can't wait!'

He found the key to the door under a flowerpot—it had obviously all been arranged. But he insisted on carrying Talia over the threshold, despite her declaring that she was far too heavy these days.

And inside, the décor, the furniture, everything, was just as she would have done it herself. 'Serine,' Dervan admitted. 'Did she get it right? She swore to me that she knew what you'd like.'

'It's perfect,' said Talia, and suddenly tears sprang to her eyes and welled over. Dervan had gone to all this trouble to please her. She felt guilty for even entertaining a shadow of a doubt where his feelings were concerned. No man would do a thing like this unless he cared very much. He had proved to her in deeds, if not words, that he loved her.

'I'm sorry,' she sniffed, when he offered her his handkerchief. 'It's just so unexpected, so lovely, so thoughtful. I must admit I'd thought about house-hunting and wondered if I'd have the energy. You've done it all for me. Thank you, Dervan. Thank you!'

There was even a nursery, furnished in pink and blue, with cuddly toys, dozens of them. And the sweetest cradle covered in white organdie. Talia stood in there for a long time.

In the kitchen the fridge and the pantry were stocked, and Serine and Paul came to visit them that evening. Serine flashed an engagement ring. 'We're not getting married yet, but Paul wanted to make sure I was his.' She looked at him adoringly, and Talia marvelled at the change in her sister.

But they had not been in the house for many weeks before Dervan started chafing about the villa development. 'I hope everything's going according to plan,' he kept saying. 'What if something happens that no one but I can handle?' He was on the phone every day, more than once sometimes. But still he worried.

'Why don't you go out there?' suggested Talia. 'I'll be all right now.' They had settled into the house and she had absolutely nothing to do.

It was obviously what he had been hoping for. 'Would you mind very much? I won't stay more than a few days.'

'Of course I don't mind, Dervan,' she smiled. They were in complete harmony again, their days spent totally in each other's company. Their lovemaking was moderated as Talia's pregnancy advanced, but he still managed to excite her and thrill her and make her feel as though she were very special.

He had bought her a new car, and Talia went out most days shopping for baby clothes. Or she would walk down to the river and sit on the bank watching the swans and the ducks, and the children playing, and the babies in prams.

One day she felt like doing neither. Her back ached and she was more tired than usual, so she sat in a chair in the garden, her radio playing softly beside her, her thoughts, as they so often were, with Dervan. What was he doing? Was he also thinking of her? Was he missing her? Of course he was. Didn't he phone every night? Didn't he tell her? But he was away much longer than he had promised. The days had stretched into a week, the week was now heading towards two. Why didn't he come home? Was he waiting until nearer the birth, as he had said he wanted to do in the first place? But that was two months away. Surely he wouldn't stay there that long?

When the phone rang Talia knew it was Dervan, calling to tell her he had booked his flight. She pushed herself awkwardly up and hurried indoors as fast as she could. But it was not her husband, it was Serine. 'Talia, how about coming over and having dinner with Paul and me? It's our anniversary—we've been engaged two whole months!'

Talia smiled into the phone. 'Thanks for the kind thought, but I don't think so. I'm feeling particularly tired today. Besides, I'm sure you'd much rather be alone.'

But Serine would not take no for an answer. 'Talia, I insist. If you don't want to drive I'll ask Paul to fetch you.'

Talia decided she was being ungrateful. 'OK, Serine, I'll come, but don't bother Paul. It's not necessary. I'm still perfectly capable of driving.'

When she left the house later that day Talia was feeling much better, but then suddenly she had a pain in her stomach so sharp that it made her cry out. It was gone again in an instant. But five minutes later it happened again, and this time she began to feel really worried and contemplated turning around and driving back home. But that would be stupid. Far better to go to Serine's where there was someone to look after her. It couldn't be the baby yet, could it? It was far too early. It was probably indigestion.

There had been a lot of traffic, but now the road ahead was clear, and Talia put her foot down on the accelerator. But suddenly the pain attacked her again, worse than ever, and she winced, closing her eyes for just an instant—and then suddenly, heading straight towards her, was a lorry.

In her moment of anguish she had swerved to the other side of the road; now she swung the wheel the other way, but not soon enough. Her back end caught the offside front of the lorry and she spun around and around, careering across the road, down the embankment, over and over. And then nothing.

When Talia awoke she was in hospital, and her first hesitant words were, 'My baby?'

The nurse smiled reassuringly. 'He's alive—just. He—'

Talia heard no more. She sank back into unconsciousness.

But the next time she awoke she felt stronger. The same nurse was standing beside her bed. So too was Serine, and Paul, both looking desperately worried.

Talia attempted to smile, and Serine started to cry. 'Oh, Talia, Talia, it's my fault! I should never have asked you to come over in your condition.'

'Who would have guessed this would happen at seven months?' asked Talia weakly. 'It was so quick. Where's Dervan? Does he know?'

Paul nodded. 'He's on his way.'

'Was he—angry with me? He told me not to drive unless I was very careful.'

'He's distraught, not angry. He blames himself for leaving you.'

Everyone was blaming themselves, but it was nobody's fault except her own. She ought to have had more sense than to take the car, feeling as she did. She closed her eyes. The effort of speaking had worn her out and she felt sore all over, though nothing seemed to be broken. She was so lucky. And the baby? Her son? She hadn't asked about him again. How was he? Was he all right. Why had no one mentioned him? She must ask—but she hadn't the strength to open her eyes or even whisper a word. Sleep reclaimed her.

It was the middle of the night when she heard a man sobbing, and her face felt surprisingly wet. She opened her eyes and in the dimly lit ward saw Dervan bending over her. They were his tears on her cheeks. 'Dervan?' she enquired softly.

He looked at her, and the pain in his eyes was more than she could stand. 'Dervan, what's wrong? Is it the baby?' Oh, God, had she killed their baby? His son? All he had ever wanted. Not her, never her—a child, his own flesh and blood, that was all he had been interested in.

'Who cares about the baby?' he muttered thickly. 'It's you who's important. Oh, Talia, I love you, I love you, *I love you.* What would I have done if you'd died and I hadn't told you? Oh, I've been so foolish!'

'Sh, Dervan, please!' Talia lifted her arms, and he knelt beside the bed and rested his head on her breast. She stroked his hair and made soothing noises, but he wouldn't be pacified.

'I thought, Talia, that it would happen again, if I told you I loved you. So I said nothing—and look what happened. I almost lost you anyway. And I hadn't told you.' His voice broke again. 'I love you so much, so very much. I always have. Oh,

Talia, Talia, please forgive me. *Please!*'

The elation coursing through Talia was indescribable. Dervan loved her! He loved her! *He had always loved her!* If she had been strong enough she would have got out of bed and danced a jig in the middle of the ward.

'I've put you through hell and I'm sorry,' he said. 'I'm an uncaring brute—I need horse-whipping. I don't deserve your love.' His face creased again with fresh anguish. 'If you'd died, Talia, I'd have killed myself. I couldn't have lived without you. You are my life.'

'But I didn't die,' she said, crying as well now. 'I'm alive, very much alive, and we have a son who, please God, will pull through as well. Have you seen him yet?'

'No, no, no, I don't care about him. It's you.' He crushed her to him. 'I'll never leave you again, Talia, I promise. I'll never let you out of my sight. I'll love and cherish and protect you to the end of my days.'

Talia swallowed hard on the lump in her throat. It was difficult seeing Dervan broken like this. He was always so strong.

'Do you think,' he asked, 'the nurse would mind if I got into bed with you?'

Talia giggled. 'She won't know.'

And so he lay beside her, and held her, and whispered words of love, and Talia wondered how she could have ever doubted his feelings for her. A baby machine! The thought was hilarious. His actions alone during the early weeks of their marriage should have told her that he cared for her deeply.

In the days that followed, both Talia and the baby regained their strength. She was soon allowed to leave the hospital, but it was the day they fetched their baby home that was their happiest moment. Dervan, who had said in his anguish that he didn't care about him, held his son proudly. They looked alike, these two Deville men, and Talia loved them both, but her own inner happiness was made complete by the knowledge that she now had someone to love her. And if it had taken the accident to get Dervan to admit it, then it was all worth while.

The publishers hope that this book has given you enjoyable reading. Large Print Books are especially designed to be as easy to see and hold as possible. If you wish a complete list of our books, please ask at your local library or write directly to: Magna Large Print Books, Long Preston, North Yorkshire, BD23 4ND, England.

This Large Print Book for the Partially sighted, who cannot read normal print, is published under the auspices of

THE ULVERSCROFT FOUNDATION

THE ULVERSCROFT FOUNDATION

. . . we hope that you have enjoyed this Large Print Book. Please think for a moment about those people who have worse eyesight problems than you . . . and are unable to even read or enjoy Large Print, without great difficulty.

You can help them by sending a donation, large or small to:

The Ulverscroft Foundation,
1, The Green, Bradgate Road,
Anstey, Leicestershire, LE7 7FU,
England.

or request a copy of our brochure for more details.

The Foundation will use all your help to assist those people who are handicapped by various sight problems and need special attention.

Thank you very much for your help.